BLESSINGS OF LOVE

THE POTTER'S HOUSE BOOKS - BOOK 15

JULIETTE DUNCAN

Cover Design by T.K. Chapin

Copyright © 2018 Juliette Duncan

All rights reserved

PRAISE FOR "BLESSINGS OF LOVE"

An interesting, unpredictable, clean romance which not only glorifies God with good sound morals and realistic imperfect characters, but it takes us on a bit of a cultural tour to a foreign mission field in Africa, specifically Burkino Faso. -*Sandra*

Blessings of Love is a well-written, faith-filled book. I loved seeing how God used missions work to change and mature the characters and how Scott and Skye's romance developed. -*Lisa*

I like the fact that was shown in this book that no matter what happens GOD loves us & willingly transforms us into new creations that He can use to reach out to reach the unfortunate. I like how this book emphasized the relationship & will of our creator can be such a blessing in our lives. -*Patricia*

A story that touched my heart with how God works in our lives when we open our hearts! -*Linda L*

Having been a medical missionary to a third world country, this story really touched my heart. I absolutely loved that both Scott and Skye were open to seeking God's direction and that Scott gained a personal relationship. Wonderful story! -*Huanne*

A NOTE FROM THE AUTHOR

Also by Juliette Duncan
Contemporary Christian Romance

The Shadows Series
Lingering Shadows
Facing the Shadows
Beyond the Shadows
Secrets and Sacrifice
A Highland Christmas

The True Love Series
Tender Love
Tested Love
Tormented Love
Triumphant Love
True Love at Christmas
Promises of Love

Precious Love Series
Forever Cherished
Forever Faithful
Forever His

A Time for Everything
A Time to Treasure

Middle Grade Christian Fiction
The Madeleine Richards Series
Rebellion in Riversleigh
Problems in Paradise
Trouble in Town

The 21 books that form The Potter's House Books series are linked by the theme of Hope, Redemption, and Second Chances. They are all stand-alone books and can be read in any order.

Be notified of all new releases by joining Juliette's Readers' list.

You will also receive a free copy of *"Hank and Sarah - A Love Story"*, a clean love story with God at the center. http://www.julietteduncan.com/linkspage/244397

NOTE: This book is set in Australia, and therefore Australian spelling, terminology, and phrasing have been used throughout.

1

Sydney, Australia

SCOTT ANDERSON CHECKED his appearance in the mirror one last time before leaving the house and smiled at his reflection. No matter how many times his pastor reminded him that humility was a virtue, he knew the Lord had blessed him.

Especially today.

Not only had he been blessed with good looks and intelligence, but he'd just received the promotion he'd been working for for months. At twenty-four he was the youngest employee at Jennings Engineering to ever hold a position of this calibre. Today was indeed a good day.

The perfect day to propose to Skye.

Scott been dating the pastor's daughter long enough to know that she was *The One*. Bright, bubbly and committed to her nursing career, not to mention, drop-dead gorgeous, Skye complemented him perfectly. Although he knew she sometimes questioned the depth of his faith, he thought she had enough for both of them.

Not that he wasn't a committed Christian, he reminded himself as he left the house and climbed into his Mazda MX-5 GT convertible he'd recently bought. Sure, maybe he could do more for his community, but he was a busy man. He'd worked hard to get where he was. You didn't graduate as a civil engineer with honours by resting on your laurels, but God had rewarded him today.

He might not be the perfect Christian, but at least he wasn't a hypocrite. *Like his father.*

One of the things Scott loved about Skye was that she was so refreshingly honest. She walked her talk, and he admired her devotion to others less fortunate than herself, even if he did sometimes think she was a bit naive. Like right now, for instance, she'd been talking about going on a mission trip. *A mission trip!* He shook his head and glanced down at the little package on the seat next to him. *Hopefully this will take her mind off it.* The box contained the most beautiful platinum and diamond engagement ring he could find. If he was going to propose, he was going to do it in style.

———

SKYE MATTHEWS GLANCED at the clock and rubbed her hands together nervously. Scott would be here for dinner any minute and her stomach fizzed with anxiety at the thought of telling him her news—and what she wanted from him. *Please Lord, soften his heart*, she prayed softly under her breath as she fingered the cross necklace hanging around her neck.

She loved Scott, she really did, and she knew her friends were envious that she was dating the most eligible bachelor, not just at church, but probably in their entire home town. Scott was the whole package—handsome, intelligent, ambitious, and he was a Christian. Well, he came to church most Sundays. He was always attentive and lavished her with flowers and jewelry. She had no doubt that life with him would be amazing.

And yet, sometimes she couldn't help but feel he wasn't committed enough. Not to her, but to God. For how could a man truly cherish anyone else if his heart wasn't fully open to the greatest love of all? She knew Scott's work was important to him and it kept him busy, but even so, she had the niggling feeling that when it came right down to it, his faith wasn't a priority. In fact, sometimes she sensed a cynicism and hardness of heart that grieved her.

Still, she reminded herself, he hadn't been raised in a loving family like she'd been. Being a pastor's kid, she'd been surrounded by love all her life. Scott's father professed to be a Christian, but it was well known that he was a bully. Scott rarely spoke about his father's behaviour, but Skye was sure that's what had hardened his heart. She truly believed that this trip could be just what Scott needed to open his heart to a life of faith and purpose. *God, You've just got to convince him to go.*

It wouldn't be easy, but Skye knew one thing. She was going —with or without Scott Anderson.

———

SCOTT FLICKED a small piece of fluff from his trousers as he stood anxiously on the doorstep of the cottage Skye shared with her friend, Fleur, waiting for her to answer. When the door opened, her bright, pretty face beamed at him in a smile that sent his senses spinning. "Wow, Skye, you look gorgeous. Hot pink looks great on you." Her hot pink jump suit matched her bright personality.

Skye flushed coyly, as he knew she would, and stood on tiptoe to kiss him lightly on the cheek. He squeezed her hand and inhaled her sweet perfume, and the aroma of something delicious cooking inside.

"Something smells nice," he said as he followed her in.

"I've made your favourite." She gave another smile, but he thought he detected a flash of nervousness in her eyes.

Does she know I'm about to propose? He fingered the ring box in his pocket, imagining her face when she opened it. "Beef and mushroom pie?" he asked casually.

"Exactly that. Sit down, it won't be long."

Skye disappeared into the kitchen as he sat at the beautifully set table and glanced around the room. It was decorated simply, with just a touch of fresh femininity. Skye had only moved out from her parents' home a year ago and now shared with a friend from her Bible study group, but Scott knew the decor was thoroughly Skye's work. She would create a beautiful home for them both to live in, he mused.

His stomach was just beginning to rumble when she brought in the pie and vegetables, which looked and smelled delicious. "What's for dessert?" he teased, thinking about the ring in his pocket and wishing he'd taken advice on what was 'proper' on these occasions. Propose after dinner, before dessert? Or after they'd finished eating altogether? And when should he tell her about his promotion?

"Let's see if you can finish your pie first," Skye teased back.

They chatted easily throughout dinner, although once again Scott thought he detected a hint of nerves in Skye's demeanour. As he swallowed his last piece of pie, she laid her knife and fork on her plate slowly, and he realised she'd barely touched her own dinner.

"Scott," she said gently, raising her gaze to meet his, "there's something I need to tell you."

"Good news or bad?" he asked in a light tone, though he was beginning to wonder if something was wrong.

"Good, I hope."

"Let's hear it."

Her gaze penetrated him like a laser. "You remember that

mission trip to build houses in Burkina Faso I was talking to you about a few weeks ago?"

He nodded slowly as dread seeped through him.

"Well, it's definitely going ahead, and I've decided to go," she continued brightly.

Scott opened his mouth to reply, but her words tumbled out. "I'd really like you to come with me." She grabbed his hand, her face filled with excitement. "It'd be such an amazing experience for us."

He couldn't believe it. *Building houses in a country no one has heard of? And in Africa, of all places!* He shook his head. "I can't take weeks off work, Skye."

"It's three months," she said matter-of-factly. Both her smile and excitement faded fast.

He let out a heavy sigh. "I can't do it."

Skye blinked as though she was holding back tears. "This is really important to me. The people over there need us. It's a real opportunity for us to live out our faith, to walk in the footsteps of the Lord." She smiled hopefully. "And it's not forever. I'd really love us to do this together."

Feeling a pang in his heart at the emotion in her voice, Scott moved his chair next to hers and squeezed her hand, the ring heavy in his pocket.

"Skye," he said, his tone soft, "I love you. I really want us to build a life together. In fact..." He went to reach into his pocket, but she cut him off, looking at him with eyes brimming with tears.

"I feel that way too, Scott. But I need to know you want the same things from life that I do. I'm definitely going on this trip, and I want you to be with me. If that's not what you want, well, I don't know how I feel about that." She gulped. "About our future."

Her words were like a blow to his heart when he realised what she was implying. His hand left his pocket with an empty palm. He felt like crying himself. Faced with the prospect of losing her, his promotion all of a sudden seemed less important. *But I've worked so hard! I can't give it all up to go on a mission trip!* His shoulders slumped. "I just don't know, Skye. It's such a big step. After the three months, then what? The company won't give me that much time off." *And I was planning on saving for the wedding of the century.*

She squeezed his hand, her expression brightening. "Isn't that the beauty of it, though? To follow our hearts and see where the Lord takes us?"

He wanted to tell her that he didn't have that much faith, but if their relationship was going to survive, he had to keep his mouth shut. Instead, he simply asked, "Can I think about it at least? Give me a few days?"

"Of course, but don't leave it too long." Although she still looked upset, there was a new determination in her voice.

LATER THAT NIGHT, lying in his bed and remembering that determination, Scott prayed with an urgency he hadn't felt for a long time, but he prayed mainly that Skye would change her mind about going on the mission trip, because the prospect of him going wasn't even an option.

———

JUST A FEW BLOCKS AWAY, Skye prayed fervently that Scott would make the right decision.

2

Scott sat at his desk the following day, staring blankly at project plans. His boss, Mike Jennings, had announced his new position that morning and everyone at the office had rallied round to congratulate him. Mike was taking the whole team for drinks after work, which Scott should have looked forward to. He was finally getting the recognition he craved.

Yet he couldn't stop thinking about Skye. Her bombshell had left everything up in the air, his carefully laid plans and vision for the future fragmented and unsure. If he didn't go on this trip, he'd lose her. If he did go, he'd lose everything he'd worked so hard for. Either way he looked at this, it seemed to be a no-win situation.

Why did she want to go to Burkina Faso anyway? Surely there were plenty of people that needed help right here in Australia. Though secretly, Scott often thought that if a person's circumstances were that dire, they must have contributed to them in some way. He'd proven where hard work could get you. He could easily have sat around moping about how tough his dad had made things for him growing up after his mum died, leaving them to fend for themselves, and used it as an excuse to not apply himself, but he'd spent his life proving everything that Dan Anderson had said about him was wrong. People made their own circumstances. But Scott knew he couldn't say that to Skye, who believed both in social justice and the transformative power of God's grace.

God's grace. Scott wanted to believe in that, he really did, but God helped those who helped themselves. Didn't the Bible praise hard work? Sighing, he rubbed at his temples, the plans in front of him a blur. If only he'd paid more attention in church. Maybe then he'd understand what Skye meant. Why her cheeks flushed in that adorable way and her eyes shone with passion when she talked about her faith.

If Scott was honest with himself, he didn't understand a lot about Skye, and last night he'd questioned whether he should just let her go. He'd never had a shortage of girlfriends, even if they hadn't lasted. He'd always treated them well, but he often felt they wanted more from him than he was prepared to give. But Skye was different. For whatever reason, she'd hung around. And she was so sweet and sunny and gorgeous, and he'd foreseen a picture-perfect future with her. With a wife like her, coupled with his new promotion, he'd be able to prove his father wrong, once and for all.

Now that Skye had hinted that their future was less than certain, however, his picture perfect vision was fast disappearing. Yet, the idea of simply replacing her with another of his female admirers abhorred him. Skye had gotten under his skin in a way no other girl ever had, and he wanted to marry her for more than just appearances. He loved her. He truly loved her, and the prospect of her leaving him twisted like a knife in his heart.

He groaned and buried his head in his hands. He was no nearer to knowing what to do.

"So, buddy, what are you going to do?"

Scott looked up, startled, as Mike's voice boomed across the office at the end of the day. *He hadn't told him about Skye's proposal, had he?*

"Do you want to drop your car home first or leave it here until the morning?"

Scott sighed with relief. Mike was talking about their planned trip to the cocktail bar after work to celebrate his promotion. He thought briefly about texting Skye to invite her, then remembered she was meeting some of her friends for coffee. In any case, she barely drank and she wasn't fond of bars. Another thing he liked about her. Scott, himself, was always too busy working to bother going, unless it was for networking purposes, and he was careful with the amount he drank. He didn't like not being in control. Tonight, though, he'd enjoy himself. He pulled on his coat and grinned at Mike. "I'll drop it home and get a taxi back later. Let's go celebrate, shall we?"

Mike slapped him on the back. "Good for you, son. You've earned it," he said, and Scott felt a swelling of pride at the older man's approval. For one night he was going to revel in his success. Skye and Burkina Faso could wait.

———

SKYE SMILED as Maria and Ellie rushed over for a hug, faces flushed with excitement. They were going on the mission trip, too, and the three girls had arranged to get together to start making travel plans. Skye had been anxious all day after her talk with Scott the previous night and had been looking forward to seeing her friends.

They met in the coffee shop attached to the church's community centre, and as they ordered lattes and a share plate, she felt her anxiety begin to subside. Seeing her own enthusiasm reflected in her friends' faces, she knew it was the right decision to go.

"We're rooming together," Maria announced with a grin.

Fresh out of Bible college, Maria had been waiting to go on a mission trip since leaving high school, and often joked she wouldn't be coming back. She was a plump girl with sparkling eyes and round cheeks, funny and warm, and Skye looked forward to spending more time with her. Maria's zest and passion for life were infectious.

Ellie was quieter and more serious. Slightly older than Skye at age twenty-three, she worked as Senior Librarian at the local high school, and in all honesty, Skye had been surprised when Maria announced that Ellie was coming on the trip, although she was glad to have her. A trip like this needed a range of talents, and Ellie's diligence and research skills had already proved useful in the planning stages.

"So, are you all ready? It's only a few weeks now." Maria leaned forward eagerly, practically bouncing in her seat.

Skye smiled to herself. She really didn't know where her friend got all her energy. "Ready as can be," she answered. "How about you, Ellie?"

Ellie grimaced. "I'm actually already packed. I was so set on getting organised that I'm living out of my suitcase and we haven't even left!"

Maria guffawed with laughter and Skye relaxed back into her chair, cupping her warm drink in both hands. "I can't wait," she said truthfully.

Ellie smiled. "I can't either. How about Scott? Did you ask him?"

Skye had told the girls the week before of her plan to invite him. The Youth Pastor in charge of the trip, Craig Holloway, had told her there'd be space in the men's bunk room, and they could certainly use someone with Scott's technical ability. Skye was hoping to get him and Craig together. Perhaps another man could inspire Scott in ways she couldn't.

"Yes, I asked him last night."

"And?" Ellie inquired.

Skye shrugged. "I don't know. He said he'd think about it, but he's so devoted to his job—unhealthily so, if you ask me. I really want him to come." An ache tore through her heart. Unless he did, their future together was uncertain.

Ellie, astute as ever, looked deep into Skye's eyes. "Are you thinking about calling it off with him if he doesn't go?" she asked quietly.

Skye drew a deep breath and nodded.

Maria shook her head, and released a soft gasp. "Really? But, it's Scott Anderson. I mean, half of the church is in love with him."

Skye shrugged. "I know. And he's a great guy, but if I'm going to spend the rest of my life with someone, I need more than a nice house and a handsome face."

Both Maria and Ellie nodded knowingly. As Christian women, they knew her struggle all too well. Eligible Christian men were in short supply.

"You have to make it clear to him," Ellie said. "He needs to tell you one way or the other if he's coming or not. Otherwise, you won't be able to concentrate on your own plans."

Skye knew she was right. "I'll tell him right now," she said with determination, and pulled her phone out of her bag.

Hi Scott, she typed. *I'm just with the girls discussing the trip. I don't want to pressure you, but I really need an answer by the end of the week, as there's a lot to plan. I'm still praying!* She hesitated for a moment. Was she being unreasonable? Perhaps he thought she was trying to manipulate him. But she wasn't. As much as she loved him, she couldn't continue their relationship if they didn't share the same passion for the Lord. It just wouldn't work. Going on the mission trip together would be a way of testing that. Scott needed to make his mind up. One way or another. She took a deep breath and pressed send.

————

As the phone beeped in his pocket, Scott sat in the cocktail bar being loudly toasted by his colleagues. The enormity of his achievement hit him, and he allowed himself to enjoy it. The youngest person to be promoted to such a position! All of his dreams and plans were coming to fruition, and he felt a nagging resentment that Skye's demands had stolen the shine from them.

He excused himself and went outside to check his phone, feeling a mixture of pleasure and foreboding when Skye's name flashed across the screen. As he read the text, his heart sank. Although her tone was sweet, he felt the same certainty he had last night—Skye was dead set on this. If he didn't go with her, he would most likely lose her.

Scott made his excuses amid protestations and back slaps from his colleagues and went home, mulling over Skye's words. Entering his house, he saw the laptop open on the kitchen table. His flatmate, Stu, must have used it and forgotten to turn it off. Leaning over, he intended to shut it off, but instead sat down and fired it up, typing the words *Burkina Faso* into the browser.

As he read, he grew more and more despondent. Skye wanted him to give up the opportunity of a lifetime to go *here?* Burkina Faso, although free of the political unrest and civil wars that blighted so many of its neighbours, was apparently one of the poorest countries in the world. Poverty and disease were endemic and the majority of homes, particularly in the rural areas, had no access to either electricity or running water. The climate was painfully hot, even for an Aussie like himself, and there were seasonal dust storms that could apparently uproot trees, and regularly did so. It looked like the last place on earth he wanted to be.

He was surprised, too, to read that the population was primarily Muslim, with a small minority of Christians. Would they even be welcome there? Were Skye and the mission team biting off more than they could chew?

He closed down the computer and sat with his head in his

hands. Despair washed over him. There seemed no way he could win. Everything in him rebelled at the thought of leaving his career to go to a country he had no desire to see, yet his heart wanted to be with Skye no matter where she went. If nothing else, her ultimatum had made him realise that he truly did love her, but now, he might lose her for good, because how in all honesty could he go to such a place? Annoyance that she was holding this over him festered inside.

3

Skye sipped on her iced latte and watched the café door, waiting for Scott. They'd both been so busy that they'd barely had time to talk on the phone, let alone see each other. She'd been wondering if he was avoiding her after receiving her text message, and had been relieved when he suggested they grab a quick coffee together on their lunch break. Tonight was Friday, date night, and no doubt he'd have some fancy restaurant planned as he always did, but she had other ideas. They were running out of time before the mission trip, and she needed an answer.

When Scott entered the café, her stomach fizzed as it always did at the sight of him, even when they'd only been apart a few hours. He was so good-looking. Tall and well-groomed, his brown eyes could melt any girl's heart. His face lit up when he saw her. Making his way towards her, he walked with that steady poise and easy confidence that she suspected was in fact partly a facade. She flushed with pride when he walked past a table of women who eyed him appreciatively, but he didn't seem to notice. His eyes were only for her.

She stood, and he kissed her on the cheek. She squeezed his

hand and smiled, feeling the slow burn in her tummy at his touch. Longing filled his gaze. She knew Scott would like to be intimate with her, but he'd never questioned or disrespected her need to wait until marriage. Another reason she loved him.

"How are you?" she asked eagerly after he'd ordered himself a drink, wondering when to broach the subject of the trip.

Scott smiled, but she saw the longing in his eyes vanish as he answered, "Busy. There's a lot going on at work."

"My nursing placement is crazy busy, too. Especially with me getting ready to leave for three months," she said, watching for his reaction. When he didn't answer and looked away, she asked gently, "Have you given any more thought to coming on the mission trip? We really need to know."

He rubbed his jaw, a habit she noticed when he was worried about something. He let out a heavy sigh. Lifted his gaze. "The thing is—I got that promotion."

"Oh, that's amazing!" Skye shrieked in delight, then instantly realised what that might mean for them.

"It is," Scott agreed, "but it's a lot of work—more than I thought with the new projects we've just secured. I can't see them letting me take three months off to help build houses on the other side of the world. In fact, it's career suicide."

Skye swallowed her disappointment. "So, it's a no?"

He shook his head. "Not necessarily. I just...I don't know. It's a really difficult decision. I want to be with you, but I've worked very hard for this. I honestly don't know what to do for the best." He looked glum, and Skye's heart went out to him. She could see how much he was struggling.

"Have you prayed about it?" she asked softly, but by the way Scott's face coloured, she figured he probably hadn't even thought about praying for an answer.

"I did that first night when you asked me, but since then, well, it just doesn't help me the way it helps you."

She took his hand. "I'm sure God was listening. He'll answer."

They sat in silence for a few moments, lost in their own thoughts and longings, then Skye bit the bullet. "The thing is, we fly out in just under two weeks, and I was thinking. I know it's date night, but it might be a good idea if we hear Craig speak about the mission. He's leading the trip and he's preaching on it tonight, and he's asking for the blessing of the church community. The whole youth team will be there and anyone from the church who wants to come. He's doing a presentation on the area, too. He's got so much more knowledge than I have. Maybe this would help you make your decision?"

As Skye had predicted, Scott looked less than thrilled. In fact, he looked as though he could think of a million things he'd rather be doing. Nevertheless, he nodded, although his reluctance was palpable. "Sure, shall I pick you up?"

"I've already arranged to meet Ellie, but you could meet us outside, about seven?"

Scott nodded and took a swig of his drink. The easy intimacy between them had disappeared, replaced by an awkward silence. Skye prayed she was doing the right thing.

———

JUST BEFORE SEVEN, Scott parked his car and walked over to the church hall, trying to muster some enthusiasm. His afternoon at the office had been so busy he hadn't had time to think, and he'd barely had time to go home and freshen up before coming straight back out to meet Skye. He spotted her standing outside the hall with her friends, Maria and Ellie, and two guys he vaguely recognised from Sunday service. With a pang of guilt, he knew that if he bothered to attend regularly, he might actually know who people were. The truth was, though he hardly dared admit it to himself, he always felt inferior next to those who were more involved in their faith. He knew he fell short in those areas, and being around people who lived and breathed it made him feel like a little boy again. He much preferred being in the office, where his competency and prestige were recognised.

It was funny, he mused as he approached Skye, that she was one of those people, and yet he never felt inferior around her. Quite the opposite. Often when he was with her, he felt she brought out the very best in him, a side he too often buried.

Skye embraced him, her joy at seeing him obvious. He wondered if she'd expected him not to turn up since he hadn't been exactly enthusiastic at her suggestion. "Hey, sweetie." She squeezed his arm. "You remember Maria and Ellie? This is Tim, he's our IT guy, and Richard, he's a builder, so he'll be our go-to practical guy. It's so exciting."

Scott shook hands with Tim, whom he thought, uncharitably, looked like the quintessential nerd, and Richard, who was the absolute picture of health and fresh-faced enthusiasm. The way he'd been standing protectively close to Skye irked Scott. A dart of suspicion streaked through him. If these guys were going on the trip, maybe he should go, if only to keep Richard away from Skye. He swallowed his jealousy and tried to make small talk, relieved when it was time to go in.

The room was filling up fast. Scott recognised Craig Holloway, the Youth Pastor, and his wife, Charlie, standing at the front. Craig held their two-year-old daughter, Teya, on his hip, and Scott wondered if she'd be going on the trip, too. It didn't sound like the best place to take a child.

They took seats near the front with the rest of the mission team, and Scott felt again that he didn't belong as everyone greeted each other with hugs and smiles. While he recognised most faces, he was at a loss to remember names or anything about them. Still, Skye was the head pastor's daughter It was only natural she should know everyone.

He was sitting between Skye and Ellie, with Richard, to Scott's annoyance, on the other side of Skye. Ellie smiled at him, seeming to notice his discomfort. She leaned in close. "It can be a little overwhelming when everyone gets together. Of course, it's fantastic we've got such a great community, but I've always preferred smaller gatherings, you know?"

Scott nodded, relieved that Ellie shared his nervousness. And he *was* nervous, he realised with surprise. His palms were moist, and his heart was racing. In most areas of life, he'd cultivated his self-confidence, but somehow in church his mask always seemed to slip.

"Are you looking forward to the trip?" he asked, half-hoping Ellie would share his reluctance there, too, but she nodded her head vehemently.

"Oh yes, I can't wait. I've wanted to do something like this for so long. It's what church should be about, isn't it? Walking in Jesus's footsteps, helping those most in need. It's far too easy to be a Christian if you never step outside your own comfort zone."

Scott felt immediately humbled. He had nothing to say to Ellie's comment. In a way, he wished he could share her and Skye's passion. It made little sense to him. Surely, God wanted His flock to acquire abundance and success. Otherwise, what was the point in hard work, in striving for a good life? He tried to tell himself Skye and Ellie were just naive, but found that, sitting there, with the growing atmosphere of anticipation in the room as Craig passed Teya to his wife and prepared himself to speak, he was suddenly questioning that concept.

Craig began with a short prayer and introduced the worship band, mostly made up of teenagers from his Youth Ministry. Scott stood with the rest of the congregation, expecting the usual Sunday hymns, and was pleasantly surprised when they struck up a rocking tune that wouldn't be out of place in the bar he'd patronised earlier in the week. Only the lyrics were different, and there was a passion to the music that Scott couldn't deny, and he soon found himself tapping his feet and singing along to the chorus. When Skye nudged him and beamed at him in delight as she waved her own hands around in time to the beat, he was surprised to realise he was actually enjoying himself.

After a few songs, Craig stepped back to the podium. Scott sat, disappointed that the music had stopped. If services were always like that, he might come to church more often. He'd had little exposure to less formal ways of worshipping growing up. His father had been strict about worship and regimented about prayer.

Someone turned on a projector and the screen in front lit up. Images of a landscape that Scott recognised as Burkina Faso flashed forward one by one in a slide show. They were the same bleak pictures that he'd found during his Internet research the other night. Craig, however, introduced the place with far more optimism than Scott had garnered from his research.

"This is Burkina Faso," Craig announced to the sea of intent faces before him, "and while it may look barren and uninviting from some of these pictures, let me assure you that is far from the case." The images began to change, showing children playing, mothers holding smiling toddlers, and proud looking men and women. Scott felt sceptical. These were some of the poorest people in the world, so what did they have to be happy about?

"In the native languages of Mossi and Dioula," Craig continued, "Burkina Faso means 'land of the upright people', and I can tell you from my own experiences—this will be my third mission trip there—that no description could be more apt. I've met some of the finest people I've been blessed to know in this country, this 'upright land'."

As images from Craig's previous trip filled the screen, he told stories and shared anecdotes about the people they'd met, funny stories about things the children had said and done, and inspiring tales of hope and faith. In spite of himself, Scott listened with rapt attention. Craig had a way with words, and his passion for that land and its people shone through in his story-telling. Not a single peep in the huge hall interrupted his voice.

Even the children accompanying their parents were listening and watching.

Craig gave a brief political and economic history of the country, and Scott found himself nodding along as Craig repeated facts he'd discovered through his own Internet research, but he delivered them in a way that told the human story behind the events. "After colonisation and ownership by neighbouring countries, Burkina Faso gained its independence in the fifties, then known as the Republic of Upper Volta. A succession of military coups ensued until the current president came to power in the late eighties. Although there has since been a period of peace and only a small amount of political unrest, the country remains subject to corruption and economic inequality, with wealth concentrated in the hands of the elite. Along with the arid soil, high unemployment, and excess mortality from disease, the people of the country are suffering."

Craig's slide show gave way to more distressing pictures of people obviously sick and in poverty, then the projector went blank and Craig read from the Bible, telling the ever-popular story of the Good Samaritan. Although Scott usually turned off mentally at this point in a service, his full attention was on Craig as he preached.

"What type of Christians are we if we walk on by?" Craig challenged. Murmurs of assent rose from the congregation, and Scott was surprised to find himself nodding along with them. Next to him, Skye leaned forward in her chair, her eyes focused on Craig. "What type of Christians are we if we stay here, comfortable in our privileged lives, and don't go to the uncomfortable places like Jesus did, if we don't share our resources like He encouraged His followers to do?" His gaze fell on Scott at that moment, and Scott was unable to look away. Something stirred inside him, although what it was, he had no name for.

Craig then began to pray. "Heavenly Father, strengthen the hearts of all who venture on the mission You've set out before us.

Soften the hearts of any who are not yet sure that this is their calling and open those hearts to Your grace. All who have questions, let them be answered in this moment. For You are the still, small voice that speaks to us in the darkness and shows us the way."

Craig had closed his eyes, but Scott couldn't tear his gaze away. A wave of emotion welled inside him, unbidden, and an ache built in his chest, as if the pastor's words were barreling straight to his core. He felt Skye's gaze on him. He turned his head. She looked at him with deep concern etched on her lovely face. "Are you okay?" She squeezed his hand.

Scott shook his head. In a way, he was the least okay and the most okay he'd felt in his entire life. He opened his mouth to try to explain, but found himself saying something very different instead. "I've made up my mind. I'm coming with you."

Skye's eyes widened and she burst into tears.

4

"You're doing what?" Mike's shock was evident from the drop of his mouth and shake of his head. "Is this some kind of joke"

Scott's stomach plunged all the way to his boots. This was going to be even harder than he'd anticipated.

Mike Jennings was in his forties, though thanks to a gruelling health regime and regular facials—not that he'd ever admit it— he looked a good decade younger. As the CEO of Jennings Engineering, he was not only Scott's main senior at the company, but a mentor and role model. Mike had taken a shine to Scott when he was just an intern fresh from college. Had helped him through his degree, fast-tracked him through his masters, and supported his rapid rise in the company. Mike had often told Scott how much he reminded him of himself, praising Scott's talents, hard work and ambition.

For Scott, Mike was in many ways the father figure he'd always longed for. One who championed him rather than put him down, who noticed his strengths rather than ridiculed his weaknesses. Scott was too proud to explain his feelings to Skye or anyone else, but he knew that letting Mike down would cost him more than his job. Losing the man's respect would cut him to the quick, not to mention prove his father's words correct. He was destined to be a failure.

Yet he couldn't let Skye down now. After his sudden announcement in church the previous evening—one he hadn't planned to make—she'd pulled him to the front to announce the news that he'd be accompanying them on the trip, and the whole congregation had prayed for him and blessed him. Craig had seemed genuinely overjoyed and Skye had been beside herself with happiness. They kissed for a long time in his car when he dropped her home. It was the most intimate they'd been, and Scott had felt deliriously happy. And surprised. If he'd thought to bring the ring, he would have proposed there and then, and he was certain that Skye would have said yes. He'd practically floated into his house, even waking Stu to tell him the news. Stu had blinked and asked if he'd been drinking. Scott just laughed.

If that was what Skye meant when she talked about being full of the joy of the Holy Spirit, then he wanted more of it. For a few blissful hours his job hadn't mattered, his father hadn't mattered, and he'd been absolutely certain that his life was on the right track.

This morning, however, the shine was gone and he felt more uncertain than ever. But he was a man of his word, and he wouldn't let Skye or the mission team down, now that he'd committed himself. Even so, he was beginning to wonder if it would turn out to be the worst decision he'd ever made, especially now that he was trying to explain himself to Mike.

"It's just for three months, Mike, and it's something I need to do. I've worked incredibly hard over the last four years. Surely I'm entitled to a sabbatical? I seem to remember Derek took one last year." Scott held his breath. Had he overstepped the mark? Derek was married to Mike's sister, after all, whereas he was just an employee. A prized one, nonetheless, but when it boiled down, that's all he was. An employee.

Mike's intense stare spoke volumes. He probably thought

Scott had gone insane. Scott wasn't entirely convinced that wasn't a factual summary.

"Derek went on a cruise for six weeks because he had high blood pressure. He didn't go off to save people for three months right in the face of one of the biggest contracts we've ever taken on! Right after I'd offered him a promotion..." Mike's face was bright red.

Scott hung his head, feeling the same as he had years ago in the face of his father's rage. His words came back... *You're no good. You'll never amount to anything. I'm ashamed of you...* Scott felt his own face growing hot. Determined not to be cowed, he raised his head and looked at Mike, opting for a conciliatory tone. "I know it's not great timing, and I should have spoken to you about it before. But it's something I have to do. It doesn't change my commitment to this company or gratitude to you for all you've done."

Mike looked slightly mollified, though he continued to shake his head in despair. "I suppose you've got to do what you've got to do. I don't want to lose you. I'll give you three months off with no pay, but I can't hold the new job offer open for you. It will go to Derek. You'll come back to your old job, and you need to be aware that this could set your career back years. I can't say how disappointed I am."

Crushed, Scott nodded. "Thank you," he said, and he meant it. Mike could have let him go and he'd come back to no job and few prospects. What company would take him on after he walked out of his last job to go build mud brick houses? Mike was offering him a great deal, yet the sting of losing his new position, especially to Derek, whom he detested because he was as useless as the expired ballgame ticket his father had given him for Christmas, was no less cutting.

Mike waved his hand towards the door. "Go on, I've got things to do. Even more, now." He huffed with exasperation.

With his heart beating in his throat, Scott left the office. He strode past his own desk, out of reception and into the sunshine. Looking out over the street, he lifted his gaze to the brilliant blue sky. His breaths came fast. "God, what have I done? If you're up there, You need to help me."

———

ACROSS TOWN, Skye was also praying, along with Maria, Ellie, Craig and Charlie. They'd met in the small room usually reserved for mentoring sessions and were offering their own personal prayers for the mission. It had been Charlie's idea, and while Scott had been invited, Skye had thought it best not to hassle him at work. She knew he was telling Mike of his decision today, and in truth there was a little part of her that worried he might change his mind.

Last night had been so unexpected, yet he'd been so sincere, so open, that Skye had no doubt she'd witnessed God's grace in a very tangible way. For a moment she'd wondered if her friends had prompted Craig to direct that particular part of his sermon at Scott, but Craig had seemed as surprised as anyone. Surprised, but pleased. A man with Scott's leadership skills and work ethic would add real value to the team. Skye had made a mental note to tell Scott about the pastor's appraisal of him.

She was so proud of him, and so excited that he was coming with her. Their future together once more seemed intact, and her heart felt like it would burst through her chest, so much so that she was barely able to concentrate on Charlie's words as she led the prayer circle... "And though the challenges we face may be great, Lord we know You will walk with us through this undertaking. Amen."

"Amen," Skye repeated dutifully, but what did Charlie mean? Although she was under no illusions that the trip would involve hard work, she was also aware that Burkina was a peaceful country and the community they would be working with were welcoming. What challenges was Charlie expecting? Skye shrugged. Perhaps it was harder for Charlie and Craig, juggling leadership as well as parenting duties.

Maybe that would be her and Scott one day. Skye allowed herself to dream. Leading missions together, being role models in the church, taking their children with them to do God's work... She brought herself abruptly back to the present when she saw Maria frowning at her. "Sorry..."

They were all looking at her, waiting for her to speak, and she flushed with embarrassment. It was unlike her to not be totally focused on prayer. She thought for the first time that having Scott on this trip might be a distraction as much as a pleasure.

"Would you like to add any prayers, Skye?" Charlie asked gently, smiling at her.

Skye nodded. "Sorry, yes, I would." She proceeded to pray for her parents, whom she'd never been away from for so long, for her father as Senior Pastor, for her patients at the hospital, and then, feeling a little self-conscious, she asked if they might pray for Scott.

Craig nodded. "Of course. A spark was ignited in him last night. Let's pray for it to grow into a slow burning fire."

Skye kept her attention firmly on Craig's words this time, and when the session finished, she felt invigorated. They hugged, and she was pleasantly surprised when Charlie asked her to walk out to the car with her. Although she always felt warm towards Charlie, she'd spent very little time with her alone and was hoping to get to know her better on the trip.

"You must be relieved about Scott's decision," Charlie said.

"Yes, totally! Something special happened last night. I'd begun to resign myself to the fact that he wasn't coming."

Charlie stopped walking and looked at her, her perfectly oval face serious. "It will be a test for you both, Skye. You know that, don't you?"

Skye frowned, thinking again of Charlie's mention of challenges in their prayer time. "You mean working together?"

"Partly, yes. I think if Craig and I hadn't already been married when we first went on a trip like this, we might never have made it." She laughed, but then grew serious again. "Conditions out there can be quite harsh, and it can be a real test of our inner resources. Even our faith. It might be particularly hard for Scott in that area."

Skye nodded. "That's why I wanted to pray for him."

"Just don't forget to pray for yourself. You're an important member of this team, too."

Skye felt worried. "Is it really so bad there?"

"It's one of the most beautiful places on earth," Charlie said, her voice soft and sincere, "and I've met the most amazing people there. But it can be a real culture shock. Life is very basic, often extremely hard. If you're not used to it...well, it can take a while to adjust."

Skye felt a little affronted. Yes, she'd led a privileged life in many ways. As the adored youngest daughter of kind and devout parents, she'd known little hardship in her life. But that didn't mean she wasn't aware of the difficulties people faced. She was training to be a nurse, after all; she looked suffering in the face every day in one form or another.

"I'm just saying to take care of yourself, too."

Skye thanked Charlie and hugged her, waving as she drove off before walking to her own car, lost in thought. It was the first time she'd thought of the trip as anything other than an exciting adventure, and Charlie's words had left her a little apprehensive. She reassured herself that she'd been guided to this point, and that she was meant to go. As for the rest, she would trust God to meet her needs.

———

THE NEXT FEW days passed in a blur of preparation, and for Scott, not a little resentment as he resumed his usual duties at work and watched Derek being primed for the role that should have been his. Every day he questioned his decision, especially when confronted with the look of disappointment Mike threw his way on a daily basis. Every day he reminded himself that the decision had been made. He wouldn't let Skye down now. Even so, the more excited Skye became as the date approached, the more doubtful he grew. He told himself that getting his ring on Skye's finger would be worth it, and he would work his way back up the career ladder in no time. He was already light years above his colleagues. While trying to ignore the anxiety that nagged at his gut, he found himself praying daily before bed, something he hadn't done with any real conviction for years, if ever, but he wasn't sure if that was a result of growing faith, or residual shock at what he'd thrown himself into. If ever he needed God, it was now.

He also wasn't getting much alone time with Skye, as most of their time together was taken up with planning for the trip along with the rest of the team. He'd found the workshop on basic building techniques fascinating, though. As he'd pole vaulted his way through the company, his job had become less and less hands on and more desk and computer bound, and part of him was looking forward to working with his hands for a change. His enthusiasm had been slightly dampened by the fact that Richard had led the workshop, and Scott was sure he'd directed most of his attention to Skye, which left him feeling overprotective and itching to claim her as his fiancée.

He'd wondered whether to propose before they flew out but decided against it. The time wasn't right, and he knew how much the trip meant to Skye. He didn't want to distract her from it. He also wanted to make sure he had her father's approval. Although John Matthews seemed happy enough that his daughter was dating him, the Senior Pastor never missed an opportunity to invite him to church events he had no intention of attending.

Scott hoped his decision to go on the mission trip would satisfy the older man. It had certainly made Skye happier, and often he thought that all the downsides were worth it to see that look of love and pride in her eyes. He just hoped the trip served to bring them together rather than widen the disparities between them in terms of their faith. For though he was trying, Scott doubted he could ever achieve the effortless trust in God that Skye displayed. And so, the remaining days passed with no small amount of inner turmoil for Scott.

Finally, the day arrived and the team stood in the airport waiting for their plane, about to embark on a thirty-three hour trip, with transits at Singapore and then Istanbul. Scott hoped there would be no delays, or it could be days before they arrived. Skye stood next to him, clutching her hand luggage with excitement, having just said a teary goodbye to her parents. Pastor John had shaken Scott's hand with a look of approval and respect Scott hadn't gleaned from him before, so he was feeling optimistic in that respect at least. The engagement ring was in his own hand luggage, tucked neatly away in the luxury gift wrapping he'd chosen.

"We're boarding!" Skye all but squealed as the announcement came over the loud speaker. She linked her arm through Scott's as they made their way towards the walkway that led to their plane. Scott's heart rate kicked up a notch when they took their seats and buckled up. He'd never been keen on flying, and there would be many hours in the air. Next to him, Skye sighed happily, leaning across him to look out the window as the plane picked up pace down the runway. Her presence helped sooth his nerves, and as the plane rose into the air, he took a deep breath. He'd done it. This was actually happening. He was going to Burkina Faso, like it or not, and a whole new chapter of his life was about to start.

Scott had yet to realise that it would turn out to be a completely new story.

5

Nearly two days later, after a long and exhausting journey, the team arrived at Ouagadougou airport in Burkina Faso. Searing heat blasted Scott the moment he stepped off the plane. A very different heat to that of Australia, dustier and oppressive, you could almost taste it. The hot dry wind came from the Sahara desert and was known as the harmattan.

They were staying at a nearby hostel for the night, and would be bussed to the small village of Teganega in the morning, the place where they'd live and work for the next few months. It had just gotten electricity, Craig had told them to Scott's relief, though he'd also said that it might not be reliable. At least tonight they'd stay in relative comfort, although Scott gazed around at the sparse room he'd be sharing with Richard and Tim and couldn't help thinking what a far cry it was from some of the luxury hotels he'd stayed in when he'd gone on company trips. Even when he'd backpacked around Bali as a student, there'd been a few more home comforts. He dreaded to think what their accommodations in Teganega would be like.

Skye bounced on her heels as she kissed him on the cheek before going off to the room she was sharing with Maria and

Ellie. "Isn't this exciting? I can't believe we're really here!" he heard her say as she walked down the corridor, arm in arm with Ellie.

He watched her go, longing for the night when they would no longer have walls and corridors between them and reminded himself this was why he was here...for Skye. He could cope with a few months of discomfort to return home with her wearing his ring. And then they could pick up where they'd left off. He'd seek a promotion at another company, though he'd return to his old job initially. If Mike thought he warranted a managerial position, so would other employers. This trip was just an interlude, he'd decided, a chance to prove himself to Skye.

He said little to the other guys as he slid into a bottom bunk and pulled the thin sheet over himself, drifting off to sleep as soon as his head hit the pillow.

THE NEXT MORNING they were bussed to Teganega. The journey took a couple of hours on dirt roads, and Scott found himself staring out at a landscape more beautiful than he'd expected, undulating hills and great cliffs of sandstone everywhere he looked. Beautiful, but harsh, a wilderness that seemed to go on forever. Next to him, Skye's gaze was glued to the window, taking everything in.

"There's Teganega!" she exclaimed when a group of low buildings appeared on the horizon. After the bumpy ride, Scott was relieved. As the bus drove down the main street, though, he wondered again at how he'd come to be here. Teganega was tiny, run-down, and filled with children. Although Craig had told them what to expect, seeing it in person was completely different.

The village had a school, several shops, and a café which had a gas refrigerator and a propane cook top. Luxuries, according to Craig. A market was held most days, which Craig said drew crowds of people from neighbouring villages and provided a great experience of local life. Scott couldn't help thinking he'd prefer a mall. The local water supply came from the nearby barrage, or small reservoir, which was in danger of running dry at certain times of the year. At other times, it was reported to have crocodiles in it.

Assembling in front of the mission house, a large but basic timber structure, Scott tried his best to look enthusiastic for Skye's sake. At least they had hot and cold running water, as well as electric fans, luxuries that many of the locals lacked. He supposed things could be much worse, but even so, he was already feeling out of place and longing for home. Three months seemed an unbearably long time to live like this.

A middle-aged man and woman, whom Scott guessed were the mission team leaders, Philip and Karen, were waiting to greet them. The couple embraced Craig and Charlie warmly and turned to the others with beaming smiles.

"Welcome! You must all be so tired!" Philip said after introducing himself and Karen. Tall and stocky, he had a stubble of a beard and a booming voice, while his wife, Karen, was the total opposite. She was petite and demure looking with a quiet voice. Even so, Scott sensed a steely strength about her.

They were offered refreshments which were gladly received by all, and then given a quick tour of the house. It was made up of a large dining hall, several meetings rooms, a kitchen, and a number of bedrooms, and a verandah that offered a view across the savannah.

As they separated to go their allocated rooms to unpack and settle in, Scott felt a pang at frustration over leaving Skye again. She embraced him, her eyes shining with happiness. He tried his best to smile sincerely.

Philip showed Scott to the room that he, Tim and Richard would be sharing with another volunteer, John, and a guy called Paul Wilson. Wilson was the chief mason, the title given to a builder in Burkina Faso, whom they'd meet at dinner. The room was tiny. Scott panicked. How would five men cope in such a small space? Being an only child, he'd never shared a room, and although he'd been house sharing with Stu for some years, they were both busy and were rarely home at the same time. He hoped Skye's room was bigger, though he suspected she'd be more used to sharing and probably less protective of her space.

Shifting his gaze from the single bed and small cupboard he'd been allocated, to his over-sized suitcase, Scott sensed Richard looking at him.

"You can use some of my space if you like. I travel light."

Scott bristled but forced himself not to glare at his room-mate who was probably only trying to be helpful. "I'm fine, thanks," Scott mumbled, heaving his suitcase onto the end of the bed. He was sweating already, and yet his skin felt dusty and dry. A fan sat in the corner of the room. He walked over and turned it on, desperate to feel some cool air. The hours sitting on the small bus had been stifling.

The fan didn't work. Scott swore under his breath and strode to the window, gazing out over yet more hills and sandstone. Feeling incredibly hot and trapped, he closed his eyes and took some slow, deep breaths. *It will be all right. I'll be all right.* He'd faced enough challenges in his life—he could do this. He *had* to do this.

Meanwhile, he tried to ignore the little voice that said this time, he might have bitten off more than he could chew.

6

Soon after arriving, the team gathered in the dining hall for their first evening meal together. Scott was feeling more disgruntled by the minute. He was far too hot, his expensive linen shirt was soaked with sweat, and to top it off, the dinner table was filled with legumes, rice and fruit. Not a decent piece of meat was in sight. How could people live like this? He anxiously looked around for Skye, but the girls hadn't arrived yet. He reluctantly took a seat on one side of a long table.

"Scott, how are you doing?" Craig Holloway sat next to him, a wide smile on his face.

Scott drew his shoulders back and mimicked Craig's smile. "Fantastic, thanks."

Craig's raised brow suggested he didn't buy Scott's enthusiasm, but before he could say any more, women's voices floated through the corridor and Skye and her friends entered the room. Wearing shorts and a sleeveless t-shirt, her hair was tied in a topknot and a few sweaty tendrils clung to her pretty face. Scott's heart lurched.

Instead of sitting next to him, she sat on the opposite side, a little further down the table with Maria and Ellie. He felt deflated, but supposed he couldn't expect to be with her every moment while they were here. Still, he felt the lack of her proximity keenly. He should have proposed when he'd the chance.

She smiled shyly at him across the table. "How's your room?"

"It's...okay," he said slowly, aware of Craig sitting next to him, listening. "The fan doesn't seem to work, though."

"Oh really?" Skye wrinkled her nose, a cute expression he always loved. "I think we've got a spare one. Maybe you could have that one?"

"Thanks," Scott said, relieved. It was funny how something as basic as a fan was suddenly coveted as much as gold dust.

The room filled up and Craig gave thanks, during which Scott tried his hardest to feel grateful for the food on the table in front of him. He tried to remind himself that many of the villagers here in Teganega probably had a lot less. Even so, he couldn't help longing for a nice steak and a dark coffee.

They tucked in, and the food tasted the way he thought it would—bland. Still, he supposed it was healthy. Skye, who had a much more nutritious diet than he did, seemed to enjoy it. She kept sneaking him little glances, smiling and fluttering her eyelashes, and he couldn't help feeling frustrated with the reality of living in the same building as her for three months with no chance of getting close. Again he thought of the ring in his bag and wished it was already on her finger.

He didn't speak much during dinner, but feigned interest in Tim and Richard's conversation, nodding here and there and hoping his yes's and no's were added at the correct times. Tim seemed more nerdy as their discussion continued, and Richard wasn't much better. At least the latter had stopped fawning over Skye, which Scott decided was one blessing at least.

After dinner, Craig announced the roster for the dishes, which on the first night would be himself and Scott. Scott tried to hide his annoyance as he followed Craig into the kitchen.

"We have to boil the water on the stove," Craig said, lifting a cannister out of the cupboard as Scott looked around for a tap.

"Don't we have running water?"

"Yes, but not always hot. In any case, we need to save it, so we use what's left over from this morning. It's okay," Craig said quickly, responding to what Scott knew was a look of disgust on his face, because disgust was what he felt. "We're boiling it, remember? It's really important to conserve water and use it frugally. We're reliant on the reservoir, and if that dries up during times of drought, life can suddenly become very, very hard."

"Like it isn't hard enough already," Scott mumbled under his breath, deliberately ignoring Craig's gaze. He stomped to the stove to boil the water, knowing he was being childish but unable to stop himself.

Waiting for the water to boil, they scraped the remaining food on the plates into the compost bin. Scott wasn't sure why he felt so awkward around Craig. Maybe it was the recollection of the compelling message the Youth Pastor had given that had convinced him to come. Or, maybe it was his ensuing resentment at being so easily convinced.

Then he remembered the sense he'd had that it wasn't Craig who'd spoken to him in church that evening, but God. He wanted to ask Craig what it felt like to hear God speaking, but he couldn't find the words. Suddenly, Scott was aware of how weak his faith was and didn't feel comfortable sharing that truth with the pastor, even though deep down he knew Craig would receive his confession with compassion.

It was Craig who spoke first as they began to wash and dry the plates and pots, making small talk about Scott's work. Although usually guarded with everyone except Skye and occasionally Stu, Scott found himself telling Craig about the promotion he'd won and lost.

"But it won't be a problem," he said as much to assure himself as Craig, "I'll get another job at the same level somewhere else."

"Maybe God has different plans for you entirely?" Craig suggested.

Scott looked at him in disbelief. "I don't think so," he scoffed, then immediately felt embarrassed when Craig raised his eyebrows, looking slightly affronted. Scott turned back to the dishes, scrubbing savagely.

Craig said quietly, "Sometimes God puts us in places and situations so we can truly see our need for Him."

Scott had no idea what to say to that and so he chose to say nothing. They finished the dishes in silence and he hurried off, hoping to catch Skye before she went to bed. He was pleased to find her still in the dining room, sitting at a table in the corner looking out the window, her eyes dreamy. He knew she was seeing this whole experience very differently from him, so far, at least.

She looked up when he walked towards her. What a captivating picture she made when her face lit up!

He felt his bad mood soothe a little. "Were you waiting for me?" he asked, smiling.

"I was indeed," she answered, a teasing lilt to her voice. "Would you like to take a walk around the village before bed?"

Scott nodded eagerly. He couldn't think of anything better. "I'd love to."

Walking outside, they headed the way they'd come on the bus, towards the reservoir. Although still hot, the heat was less intense, which made walking a little more bearable. As they strolled through the village, the surreal nature of the situation hit Scott. Just a few weeks ago he'd been in Australia with all the creature comforts his life entailed and absolutely no notion of leaving. Now, he was here, with nothing but a suitcase full of clothes.

And Skye.

When he gazed at her, he noticed the shadows under her eyes. It had been a long few days for both of them.

"How are you finding it?" she asked. When he hesitated, she continued, "Be honest."

He grimaced. She knew him too well. "It's been a shock. I thought I knew what to expect, but now that we're here, it's hit me just how different it is from Australia."

Nodding, Skye looped her arm through his as they walked, but Scott saw the flash of disappointment on her face and felt annoyed. *How did she honestly expect him to feel?* Who in their right mind would be jumping for joy at the chance to live this way and in this heat? A young village boy crossed the road in front of them, singing, in spite of his threadbare clothes and obvious undernourishment.

Scott shook his head. "Honestly, it's like some kind of weird, topsy-turvy world." He paused. Drew a breath. "I guess it makes me feel lucky for what we've got at home." He didn't add the thought that he wished home was exactly where they were right now.

"We're very blessed, Scott," Skye said, "and I think it's only right we share some of those blessings. Especially as Christians. That's what our Lord did, isn't it, taught us to share? Even *you* must remember the loaves and fishes story from Sunday School," she finished, giving him a playful nudge.

"Of course I do. I did pay some attention." Though he remembered thinking as he got older that a miracle such as that could never happen today. People were out for what they could get, and the only way was to look out for number one and make sure you took what you wanted from life because no one else would see to it. At least, that's what his dad had told him, and Scott believed him.

He felt morose until Skye tugged on his arm. "Look, isn't it pretty?" she exclaimed, and Scott realised they were nearly at the reservoir. It was just a lake, surrounded by scrub land that was admittedly lusher than the rest of the landscape. Across from them, a large bird he didn't know the name of, ducked its graceful head to drink. Feeling the coolness coming off the water, Scott felt himself soften a little.

"It's nice here at this reservoir," he admitted. It was great spending some time away from the rest of the team and alone with Skye. Sitting at the edge of the lake, he put his arm around her shoulders. When she dropped her head onto his shoulder, he inhaled the smell of her hair, the familiarity of it soothing him.

"I'm so glad you're here," she said, gently stroking his arm.

Scott gazed around at their surroundings and at the fast approaching sunset, spreading golden fire over the sky, blurring where the sky met the land. The colour and shade did offer a fierce kind of beauty, and he was glad to share this moment with Skye. Except, if he'd ever envisaged sitting with her gazing out at an African savannah, it would have been in the context of some luxurious safari holiday. *Not a mission trip.*

He dropped a kiss on the top of her head. "I'm glad, too," he said, but his voice caught on the lie.

Skye stiffened a little in his arms, then she sighed and relaxed again. "I know this isn't easy for you." She traced a line up his bare arm.

"It's easier when I'm with you," he said truthfully.

She smiled up at him. He tipped her chin with his hand, moving in to kiss her on the lips, but she gave him her cheek, then pulled away to snuggle into his arms again. He tried again, but she jerked away.

"What's wrong?" he asked, hurt at the rejection.

"It doesn't feel right. We're not on a date, we're here to work. As Christians. And you know I want to wait."

"It was just a kiss. I've always respected your boundaries, you know that." Scott's jaw tightened.

"Then respect them now," she said firmly.

He nodded, but he truly couldn't understand why they couldn't at least share a kiss. The moment was gone. They returned to the house in silence, alone with their thoughts. Scott walked her to her room and stood awkwardly, wary of even kissing her on the cheek.

Instead, she embraced him. "I'll see you tomorrow. I hope you get a good sleep."

He left her without responding and shuffled to his own room, frustrated, hurt and fearing that instead of this trip being the way to keep Skye, it could be the very thing that separated them.

————

SKYE PLOPPED ONTO HER BED, dejection weighing heavily on her heart.

Maria looked over from her bunk, a book in her hands. Setting the book down, she crossed the room and sat beside her. "What's wrong, Skye? Are you and Scott okay?"

"I'm not sure." She sat up and leaned against her pillow. "We went and sat by the lake, and it was lovely, but I could tell he's not happy. I think this place is a bigger culture shock than he expected."

"Do you think he'll go home?"

Skye's eyes widened. She'd never considered that a possibility, but now wondered if he might. What if he wanted his life back more than he wanted to be with her? She brought her knees to her chest and hugged them, in spite of the heat, and tried to see through her fear. God wouldn't have inspired Scott to come just for him to give up at the first hurdle. He was also a man of his word. No, he'd see the project through to the end, but at what cost to their relationship? Maybe she'd been wrong in asking him to come.

She said as much to Maria, who put her arm round her. "It *is* only the first day. Trust God. It will work out," she said, but for once that simple and eternally true advice didn't comfort Skye as it usually did.

Maria's arm felt hot and heavy around her shoulders, so she

wriggled away, trying not to be unkind, and went to the small wash basin to wash her face. She used as little of the water as she could, which wasn't hard, since it came out little more than a drip. They were only supposed to shower once a week, and she already felt horribly sticky and unclean. It was fair to say she would miss home too, but she tried to remind herself of the reason she was here—to devote at least part of her life to caring for the most vulnerable of God's people. Although her nursing career would enable her to care for people, of course, she'd had a real desire to break out of her privileged bubble and do what she could to help those of God's people she wouldn't usually come into contact with. She knew it would be hard, and so she understood that, without that same depth of motivation leading Scott here, he might well be having second thoughts.

Skye got into bed and prayed, once again, for God to soften Scott's heart before she lost it.

7

Scott came down for breakfast still feeling out of sorts, and when Skye sat apart from him again, he began to feel really fed up. Tim and Richard chattered annoyingly beside him about the day ahead, and as Richard shared some of his basic knowledge about construction work, Scott fought hard not to roll his eyes. Instead, he smiled politely.

They had a short devotion after breakfast, and he was pleased when Skye rushed to his side and sat next to him. More than pleased—relieved. He'd spent a sweaty and unsettled night tossing and turning, replaying their conversation the evening before and the moment Skye had refused his kiss.

Charlie led them in a simple morning prayer, and then Craig got up to speak. Scott tensed. The last time he'd experienced Craig's preaching, he'd been influenced to come here, and he didn't want to feel out of control again.

But when Craig read a Bible verse Scott hadn't heard—or didn't remember hearing—before, the story of the potter and the clay, he realised its relevance to the day ahead, and his ears pricked up in spite of himself.

This is the message that came to Jeremiah from the Lord: "Jere-

miah, go down to the potter's house. I will give you my message there."
So I went down to the potter's house and saw him working with clay at
the wheel. He was making a pot from clay. But there was something
wrong with the pot. So the potter used that clay to make another pot.
With his hands he shaped the pot the way he wanted it to be.

Craig closed his Bible and looked up. "God is like that potter,"
he said, "and we're like that piece of clay. If things go wrong in
our lives, it's not the end, because God does what that potter did
with his clay. He gives us a second chance. He doesn't give up on
us. No, because He loves us so much, He gives us a completely
fresh start.

"Some of you haven't been on a trip like this before, and you
might be wondering what you're doing here. You could call it a
fresh start, a new venture, or even a new 'pot'."

Scott's heart quickened. He was definitely wondering what he
was doing here. Craig seemed to have the uncanny ability to
speak words that hit the mark. He shared passages from the Bible
that would make little sense if Scott had read them on his own.
But Craig brought the stories alive, making them meaningful and
relevant to everyday life. Skye had said on one of their first dates
that the Bible was a living scripture to be engaged and wrestled
with. He'd always found it rather dusty and dry and struggled to
relate much of it to his life. Listening to Craig, he began to understand what Skye meant.

"God only wants what's best for us. Even though we have free
will to make our own choices in life, if we're pliable in His hands,
just like the clay in the potter's hands, He can make something
beautiful out of our messed up lives.

"But God is at work in us for His good pleasure, not our own.
He owes us nothing, but because of His great love for us, He
freely extends to us compassion, mercy, grace, and a second
chance.

"Later this morning, as you begin to work with the bricks
made out of dirt that would normally be deemed useless, and

you build houses from them that will enrich the lives of many in Teganega, keep this in mind. Just like the dirt being used to make houses, God can take what seems useless and create something beautiful and of infinite value from your life.

"I'd ask each of you to search your hearts. Are you allowing God to work in your life? To fashion and shape your thoughts and attitudes to align with His? Or are you quarrelling with Him and questioning what He's doing with you?

"God has created each of us to be unique and special. It's our responsibility to take the talents He's given us and use them for His glory and pleasure. In doing this, we find ultimate fulfillment in life. Rather than living with disappointment and dissatisfaction with what God has or hasn't given us, we can choose to thank Him in everything and for everything. Just as the clay finds its greatest purpose when it stays pliable in the potter's hands, so our lives fulfill their highest and greatest purpose when we allow our Potter to have His way with us and we become what He truly intended us to be from the beginning, using our gifts and talents for Him."

Craig's words pierced Scott as he thought about his own gifts and talents. He hadn't been using them for God. Rather, he'd used them to get ahead, to become successful, to prove his father wrong.

"Yet we must never forget that we don't do it alone," Craig continued. "While we make our own free choices in life, by trusting in God and living by His grace and example in Jesus, we find those choices become aligned with the purpose that God has fitted us for. The real question is, and I'll give you this to ponder as you work with your own clay today, and I ask myself this question as well, are you giving yourself into God's hands, to be fashioned as He wills? Or are you dry and hard, and resisting His hand on your life?"

A hushed silence fell on the room. A few of the local masons shouted 'Amen'. Scott felt even more confused, and even anguished, though those were feelings he usually swallowed and avoided. He knew it was because he didn't know how to place himself into God's hands, to have that deep and radical trust and faith that both Skye and Craig had. He always tried so hard to be successful, yet when it came to faith, he felt as though he didn't have a clue.

However, when Philip Carmody got up to speak about the work of the day ahead, he began to feel better. The practical stuff, now *that* he could understand.

"I'd like to formally welcome all who are newcomers here to Teganega, and to our mission house," Philip began. "Thank you to Craig for a challenging message this morning, and I would echo it by saying to our new arrivals that you may think you're here on mission to help the locals, but you'll find that you are in fact truly here so that God may work on you and indeed fashion you. No one leaves Burkina Faso unchanged."

Another chorus of 'Amens' sounded from the local masons.

"In truth, this project is not so much about *helping,* as *empowering.* As you're learning to build the vaulted earth brick houses, using an ancient Nubian technique adapted for the region, you'll also be instrumental in helping to train the apprentice masons to become entrepreneurs, so that they might go on to earn an income for themselves and their families, while at the same time providing more people in Burkina with safe and comfortable homes. We're helping to build a sustainable market that will have far-reaching, positive effects."

Scott's interest grew as Philip talked about sustainability and the design of the houses, which were specially designed to be safe, to regulate temperature, and to be comfortable, yet still affordable for all. He had skills that could come in incredibly useful. For the first time, Scott understood the importance of this mission. It wasn't just about building a few mud brick homes. He would be part of something real, something that could bring sustainable change.

Philip split them into their teams. Scott was relieved when Skye was placed on the same team as him. He flashed her a genuine, excited smile. She beamed back at him, and their gazes locked for a moment before they returned their attention to the task at hand. Paul Wilson was their chief mason, and Tim and John, the other volunteers on the team. Richard was assigned to a team with Maria and Ellie, which Scott couldn't help but be pleased about.

Philip introduced them to the two local apprentice masons who would be working with their team, Noufou and Yacouba. The two men nodded, and Scott was struck by the pride and warmth emanating from them. He recalled the young boy he'd seen yesterday evening. He could hardly generalise, as he'd been here such a short time, but every local he'd met so far carried an air of humble confidence and cheerfulness that challenged him.

As they headed out with their tools to begin the day's work, Scott realised he was looking forward to it. He felt a similar buzz to the one he experienced when starting a new project back at his workplace. A place that was beginning to seem incredibly far away.

———

As they drove through the town towards the work site, Skye looked out of the work vehicle, a battered van that she thought could break down at any minute, and smiled at the children who played outside their houses. She was delighted when some of them waved at her.

"Have you noticed everyone seems so friendly here? I wish it was like that back home," she said.

Next to her, Scott shrugged. "Yeah. A bit. I still don't understand how they look so happy when they're playing in dirt, though."

Skye shook her head at him. "Honestly, Scott. Children don't need fancy things to be happy. My cousin's children are at their happiest in the mud, no matter how many toys she buys them. Children are simpler than us. More innocent."

"More naïve, I'd say."

She gave up and went back to looking out of the dusty window. Sitting behind them, Tim joined in their conversation. "Jesus said we must become like little children in order to enter eternity." He spoke with an air of pomposity that made Skye want to giggle. Next to her, Scott bristled, but thankfully didn't respond. She hoped he wasn't going to get into conflict with anyone on their first day at work. He was used to working in what she imagined was a fairly ruthless environment, after all.

Pulling up at the work site, they gathered to receive their instructions from Paul. Looking at the building site and the huge pile of mud bricks that had been made ready for them to use, Skye fingered the cross around her neck and prayed silently for strength. Craig had given them all some rudimentary training in the days leading up to the trip, and assured them it was simple enough, but now that she was actually here, facing this huge pile of bricks, she suddenly felt out of her depth. She was used to nursing, not building. What had she been thinking?

At least Scott looked more at ease. She'd noticed him growing more attentive during Philip's speech, and he was giving Paul the same attention, his gaze focused as he absorbed the instructions. He was in familiar territory now.

They started work. Skye soon felt overwhelmed as she struggled to keep up with the others, though she was too proud to admit it. The sun shone down relentlessly, and as it drew towards midday, she strained even more, her limbs aching from the physical work and the heat. It was so hot, the air was thick, and it was hard to even take a deep breath without her lungs burning. Only Noufou and Yacouba seemed unperturbed, and as a result seemed to work twice as hard as everyone else. When it was time for a break, they were the only ones who didn't look exhausted.

"Does the heat ever get too much for you?" she asked Noufou as she wiped her brow with her arm.

He smiled at her, his eyes kind. "Yes. When it gets hotter than this, we mostly stay inside and pray for the rains to come."

"It's okay if you need to take a break, Skye," Paul said, looking at her with sympathy.

She shook her head. She'd been so eager to come, so she wasn't going to give up on the first day. But it rankled that Scott seemed to be handling the physical activity and heat so much better than her. He even seemed to be enjoying himself, asking Paul questions and getting involved in the intricacies of the project.

As the afternoon wore on, however, they all grew slower and more tired and Scott made mistakes. He looked mortified when Paul had to correct him. Skye tried to catch his attention to show sympathy, but his jaw was set. and eyes focused fiercely on the task at hand. She knew it hurt his pride to have his mistakes acknowledged and then corrected. It had probably been a long time since he'd experienced not being brilliant at everything he did. As much as she knew humility was a virtue, she did hope it wouldn't come too hard for him.

Skye was ready to drop by the time Paul said it was time to finish, before the day reached its hottest point. They were all quiet on the ride home. Her eyes and head drooped. If it wasn't for the stifling heat making it hard to breathe, she would have fallen asleep in the van.

Before the team went to their rooms for a rest before the evening meal, Tim suggested they take a walk together after dinner. Skye concurred. It'd be nice for them to bond, but she caught the flash of disappointment in Scott's eyes and realised she'd made a mistake by voicing her agreement. He'd probably been hoping for time alone with her, especially after things had been so strained last night. She bit her lip as he walked with her to her room in silence.

"It'll be nice to go for a walk with the others, won't it?" She squeezed his hand, hoping to convince him.

Scott smiled, stifling a yawn, and dropped a kiss on her forehead. "Sure. See you later, hey?"

She returned his smile, but the aloofness of his response left her cold. All she could do was trust, like Maria had encouraged her to do the previous evening.

AFTER DINNER, the group went for the walk as planned, although everyone dragged their feet. Although Scott was quiet, Skye was relieved that he'd come and appeared to be in a slightly cheerier mood than earlier. No one had enough energy for a long walk and they soon agreed to return to the mission house and sit on the verandah out back in the shade.

She enjoyed the relative coolness on the verandah and sipped on the bottled water Paul distributed to everyone. Snacks and bottled water were rationed due to low supplies, making it all the more real that they were indeed in a third world country.

She turned her head and smiled at Scott. Guilt over pushing him away last night sat heavily on her heart. She craved his closeness as much as he no doubt craved hers, but last night, it just hadn't felt right. Everything here felt so different, and while she was unsure what this trip would truly mean for their future, she was cautious about getting too physically close to him.

Occasionally she thought about marriage, about being Mrs. Scott Anderson, but in truth, they'd never even spoken about it, except at the beginning of their dating when she'd made it clear she intended to keep her virginity until marriage. He'd accepted her vow and continued to get close to her, even coming all the way to Burkina Faso rather than losing her, so he must be thinking about it too, surely? Sometimes she wished she was able to read his mind.

Paul cut through her daydreaming. "So, Scott, how did you find your first day? You've been very quiet."

"Tiring," Scott said with a yawn, which made the rest of the group laugh. "And intense. But also interesting. I like learning new things."

Paul nodded, looking impressed. "You've got a great skill set to bring to this project. I'm glad you're finding it interesting. How about you, Skye? You seemed to struggle a little earlier."

She blinked. Had her ineptitude been that obvious? She didn't want to be the weakest member of the team, especially as she was the only woman. "It was hot," she ended up confessing, "and it was a little overwhelming. But I'm sure I'll get used to it."

"Me too," Tim chimed in. "It was such intense work. So different from sitting in front of a computer in an air-conditioned office!"

Scott laughed at that, nodding at Tim. "Tell me about it. I get sick of sitting in an office, especially since I moved into management. It was good to be working with my hands again."

Tim spread out long, white, soft looking fingers. "I've never worked with my hands in my life. Mum keeps telling me I've got piano player's hands. They'll be raw with callouses by the time I get home."

Scott laughed again and as the two of them got into a discussion about their previous workplaces, Skye watched in amusement. It was the first time Scott had really made an effort to get on with the rest of the team, especially Tim, and she felt a warm glow of pride. He was really trying. She could see that.

Paul announced he was going to bed and Tim and John followed, leaving Scott and Skye alone. He looked at her, a question in his eyes, before she scooted her chair closer to his. "You seem happier," she said.

Scott gave a wry smile. "I don't know if 'happy' is the right word, but I'm trying to make the best of it since we'll be here for a while. I don't want to spend the whole time being entirely miserable."

Skye smiled and reached for his hand, entwining it in hers. He raised her hand to his lips, kissing her palm with the lightest of touches. She closed her eyes and dropped her head onto his shoulder. Maria had been right—she just had to trust God. Scott and she were here for a reason, she had no doubt about it.

As he stroked her hair, she relaxed, releasing a long exhale that seemed to carry all the tensions of the day along with it. She allowed herself to enjoy being near him, to enjoy the moment without worrying what the future might hold. *Commit your way to the Lord; trust in Him and He will do this: He will make your righteous reward shine like the dawn, your vindication like the noonday sun.* Her heart warmed. God knew what she needed before she even knew herself.

She must have nodded off because the next thing she knew, Scott was lightly shaking her, laughter in his voice. "Come on, sleepyhead, let's get you to your room."

He walked her upstairs and left her with a light kiss on her forehead. She smiled and watched him walk away before stepping into her room quietly. Maria and Ellie were already in bed and the light was off. She carefully removed her shoes and changed into her night attire before collapsing onto her bunk. As she drifted off to sleep, mud bricks and the happy faces of children playing in mud filled her mind.

8

As expected, the following days brought more hard work and unbearable heat. Despite that, the houses came along quickly, and Scott enjoyed rising to the challenge. There was a certain simple satisfaction in building, and in being part of a creation rather than merely planning and designing it on a computer. Most days, the hours passed quickly. So absorbed in his work and in the flow of creating, time just slipped away. There was, he'd discovered to his own surprise, a freedom in the work that he'd never experienced back home.

Even more freeing...he wasn't seeking anyone's approval, wasn't worried about impressing anyone, or using the project at hand to get ahead. For the first time in his adult life, he wasn't striving for more and more success, and rather than feeling like a failure, he felt the most fulfilled, the most useful, he ever had. The almost constant background noise of his father's criticism, which he'd always perversely used as a spur to get ahead, was silent here, blown away by the dusty winds.

Not that he didn't struggle. At night, the heat made it difficult to sleep, even though he was physically exhausted. And he still felt out of place when he had to socialise with the team. Trying to understand this country and its people was the biggest challenge. No matter how much he enjoyed building the mud houses, it baffled him that the people could be so happy with them. He knew, of course, that they had little choice, given the poverty the area faced. To many here, the small houses were like palaces. What he couldn't understand was how they carried on with life with so little. They lived, loved, and laughed in the midst of such hardship.

He asked Craig one night when it was again their turn to do the dishes. Craig took his time replying, but when he did, he spoke in measured tones. "Perhaps because things are so hard here, it makes life so much more intense. The smallest luxury becomes a blessing. I always find that the less 'stuff' people accumulate, the more able they are to focus on the things that really matter."

Scott frowned. "That's what I don't get. This idea that you have to be poor."

Craig angled his head as he wiped a plate. "Where did you learn that?"

Scott cringed, realising how little he truly knew about the faith he outwardly professed. "Well, don't monks take a vow of poverty? And all the stuff about rich men and the eye of the needle?"

Craig smiled gently at him. Scott felt like a child, learning things for the first time. He felt uncomfortable, although he listened attentively to Craig's words. "Monks make a choice to live that way. I imagine that's very different to being forced to live in poverty.

Scott shrugged. "I guess so."

Craig picked up another plate and began wiping it. "I've always seen the scripture about the rich man as a warning not to hoard wealth, not to place the accumulation of worldly things before God and service to our fellow men and women. I believe that it's the hoarding of wealth and the addiction to status accompanying it that causes systemic poverty." Folding his arms, Craig leaned against the counter and crossed his ankles. "There's more than enough wealth to go around, but most of it is in the hands of a few because essentially, man's heart is wicked. So, no, I don't believe that the poverty here or anywhere is a good thing, which is why we must work to relieve it."

Scott mulled over Craig's words. They kind of made sense, but left him with a sense of guilt at the same time.

Craig continued. "Jesus came to reach the homeless and the hungry, not because there's any virtue in these things, but because God is compassion. He wants those who follow Him to also show compassion to those who are suffering, but when people concentrate on wealth and status, what room is there for others less fortunate than themselves in their hearts?"

Scott was unable to reply. He felt somehow rebuked, even though Craig's tone was only one of wanting to help, to explain, as per his role of pastor. But Scott knew he was like the young rich man in question. He chased status. He hoarded wealth in terms of spending it on beautiful things, designer watches and the best restaurants. And he'd never been one to worry about those who had less. He tossed a few loose coins in the collection plate when he went to church, and gave a small percentage to charity through a company scheme, but he had to admit that was more for appearances than anything else.

Later that night in his room, he looked at the Bible he'd placed next to his bed. Again, more for appearances than anything else. Every night, Tim, John and Paul picked theirs up before kneeling to pray. Most mornings, they did the same. Scott was sure it hadn't gone unnoticed that his was barely touched, and in fact, it was gathering dust. There was almost a resistance in him to picking it up, as if it would take him somewhere he wasn't sure he was ready to go. He enjoyed Craig's brief morning devotions, and the pastor's wise words gave him much to think about, but he hadn't had the feeling he'd experienced back in

Australia when he'd been swept up into something larger than himself and had agreed to come on the trip. He didn't know which was truer—the yearning to feel that again or wishing he'd never experienced it at all.

As a result, when Sunday came, he felt agitated. Rather than staying in the mission house for worship as he'd assumed they would, Philip announced they were going to the village church. The idea didn't thrill Scott, but Skye was excited, as he knew she would be. She'd been unusually quiet the last few days, and he sensed she wasn't enjoying the building work at all, although she brushed him off whenever he tried to help.

As they arrived at the church, Scott wasn't really surprised to find that it was even more basic than he'd expected. It was a large breeze block building with timber benches. Handmade musical instruments such as tambourines and *djembes,* rope-tuned skin-covered goblet drums played with bare hands sat on a small stage. There were signs on the wall, in both French and the local languages. *Jehovah Shammah, El Shaddai.* He made a mental note to ask Craig or Skye what they meant.

It was also incredibly hot and crowded. The whole village, it seemed, had turned up, and countless children played and happily ran around with no one reprimanding them. Despite the heat, the atmosphere, was one of anticipation and optimism. There was nothing sombre about this church. Wondering what to expect, Scott glanced at Skye, who shrugged with a bemused expression on her face.

The Burkinabe pastor, a solid, middle-aged man, beamed at the congregation and shouted something Scott couldn't understand. The locals in the crowd shouted back, including Noufou and his wife who stood next to himself and Skye. Scott's heart sank when he realised the service wasn't in English, then reprimanded himself. *Why on earth would it be?* Again he realised how he saw the world through his own lens.

To his surprise, the pastor invited some of the children, who were holding a range of instruments, onto the makeshift stage. They gathered in a circle and began to dance, singing exuberantly and shaking their tambourines and banging their drums. The beat increased and many of the congregation began clapping, whooping and stamping their feet. The pastor danced around the stage in time with the children, raising his arms and face to the sky, shouting out choruses of 'Amens.' Scott had never seen anything like it. This was nothing like the church he was used to, or his conception of what worship was,. Generally, services were boring affairs to be suffered through with as much politeness as possible. The people here treated worship in a completely different way. This was a celebration, a rejoicing.

All the exuberant emotion made him uncomfortable. Next to him, Noufou had risen to his feet and was dancing away, and to Scott's amazement, all the locals joined him. And then Skye stood, a look of rapture on her face as she swayed from side to side and raised her arms to the ceiling. Scott gazed around. All the other team members were on their feet too. Charlie bounced Teya on her hip and waved her other hand in the air. Even Tim shuffled awkwardly from side to side. When Scott caught his gaze, he gave an embarrassed grin. Scott smiled back wryly, then returned his attention to the stage. He realised his foot was tapping in spite of himself.

The pastor began a call and response to the crowd as the children went into a different song, and Scott wished he knew the language and the words. In a way, though, he understood that for Skye and the others, it didn't matter. The atmosphere spoke for itself.

Scott longed to get up and join them, a thought that left him stunned, but he couldn't break through his own resistance. He didn't want to make a fool of himself, even when he knew that was only his own misplaced pride. Everyone else was too busy enjoying themselves. If anything, he stood out more by sitting.

Not wanting to look silly, he bowed his head and clasped his hands together so people would at least think he was in prayer.

Amidst the singing, dancing and shouting, peace settled over him like a comforting blanket, and he became aware of a sense of being held. Of being known. Startled by the strange senses, he waited for them to pass, but they only intensified. A wave of sadness rose in him, brought tears to his eyes. He blinked them away fiercely.

The sense that he was being held, being cared for, increased further. *It's okay, Scott, I'm with you...*came an awareness inside. Not a voice, exactly. It was as if the words, *the knowing*, had always been there, but he was only becoming aware of it now. For a moment, he closed his eyes and relaxed into the presence, but as the emotion bubbling inside threatened to overwhelm him, he opened his eyes sharply, sat up straight and pushed the feelings away. It was just the noise and emotion in the room, he told himself. He was getting carried away by it.

He was relieved when the music ceased and the pastor gave a sermon that was mercifully short, since he couldn't understand a word of it. Next to him, Skye looked radiant, as if the dancing had invigorated her. She looked so beautiful, her hair in a ponytail, clad in a simple white t-shirt and linen shorts, with not a scrap of make-up, which was probably pointless in this heat. It was funny, but before Skye, he'd always preferred his girlfriends to be polished, girls who spent hours on their hair, make-up and nails. It went with the image he tried to portray. But Skye was both naturally beautiful and refreshingly unconcerned about how she looked.

Following the sermon, a few of the local women, including Noufou's wife, led a short hymn in the gospel style. Noufou watched her with obvious pride, and Scott wondered if that could be him one day, watching Skye.

Afterwards, everyone milled around, greeting and blessing each other. Scott hoped to get away for a walk with Skye, and was about to suggest it when Noufou approached them. "This is Femke," he said, introducing his wife proudly. "Some of us are having lunch outside under the acacia trees. There's enough to go around. We would like it if you could join us."

Scott hesitated, trying to find a polite way to refuse, but Skye nodded enthusiastically. "How lovely! Yes, we'd love to eat lunch with you, wouldn't we, Scott?" When she turned to him and pleaded with her eyes, he had no choice but to agree.

9

Still exhilarated from the service, Skye made her way, along with a reluctant Scott, to the grove of acacia trees to share lunch with Noufou and Femke. She'd embraced the wildness and the passion of the service, had felt the presence of God in a visceral, embodied way that had reinvigorated everything she already knew to be true, and her heart was still singing.

After the last few days, she'd been badly in need of a lift. Though she in no way regretted her decision to come to Burkina Faso, each day was proving physically harder and more frustrating. And it wasn't only that she found the building work hard. She felt that it wasn't what she was meant to do. At night, when Maria and Ellie were sleeping, she got out of bed and prayed, seeking clarity, for a clear sign of the way forward, but nothing had become apparent. She kept thinking back to Craig's sermon about the clay and the pots, and had the distinct feeling that somehow she wasn't working on the right pot.

It was the same with her nursing career back home. She loved being a nurse and knew that God had called her to the work, but still there was a sense of something missing. Especially when she spent more time doing paperwork than caring for people. She never felt that she had enough time to truly get to know her patients, to see them as people with stories and lives and loves, rather than bodies waiting to be attended to.

There was something about being here, about the starkness of the landscape and the brutal heat, and the intense simplicity with which the people lived their lives, that pared everything down to the bone and made her question everything about herself, and that made her uneasy. Although she was glad Scott was starting to find his feet, she couldn't help but feel a little resentful. Not only were they barely getting to see each other, he was becoming immersed in the work and was contributing so much to the project, while she found every day a struggle and made many mistakes. Although Paul was too kind to say so, she was sure she was slowing the team down.

The irony of it hadn't escaped her—that she was struggling when she'd been the one so desperate to come, while Scott had made peace with the situation and was, to use his words, 'making the best of it.' She almost felt like a hypocrite. While she'd preached about the importance of mission and of living out one's faith, here she was, feeling like it was all too much. Although she was trying her best to keep her spirits up, she knew the others were noticing. Maria and Ellie kept asking if she was all right, no doubt assuming her low mood was because of Scott.

Just the day before, Charlie had approached her after breakfast when she was going for a shower and rubbed her arm. "Hi, Skye," she'd begun, gently pushing Teya's sticky hands off her shorts. "How are you? We've been so busy I've barely had a chance to talk to any of you guys this week." Charlie had been building too, taking it in turns with Craig to look after Teya. Skye didn't know how they managed to combine working like this with looking after a child, but she supposed it was easier when there were two of you.

"I'm great," Skye responded with her usual enthusiasm, but she could hear her tone of voice betraying her. Teya raised her arms for a hug. Skye picked her up, breathing in the child's sweet scent.

"Okay, I'm not so great,' she confessed. "I'm finding it really, really hard. I keep making mistakes on the site and I'm sure the guys are getting sick of me, and I just feel so...I don't know, almost out of sorts with everything. Still, it's early days. I'll get used to it."

Charlie had smiled at her with obvious sympathy and Skye thought back to their conversation back home.

"You did warn me that this wouldn't be all fun and games. Now I see what you were preparing me for."

Taking a wriggling Teya from her arms, Charlie gave Skye a warm hug. "I'm here if you need to talk."

Skye appreciated the offer, but could Charlie, who seemed to move so effortlessly through life, really understand?

As if reading her mind, Charlie continued. "You're not the only one to question a calling. Ask Craig. I was ready to leave him and the whole church when Teya was a few months old."

"Really?" Skye's eyes widened.

Charlie nodded. "Yes. I resented being at home all day while Craig got to carry on doing whatever he wanted, and I really grappled with my identity and with what God wanted for me. I talked with a few of the church elders but was told that being a wife and mother is basically a woman's role in life and I should accept it, and that was that. I was so shocked that I considered taking Teya and walking away from everything and everyone."

"What happened?" Skye asked, fascinated.

"I couldn't go. I kept praying, even though I didn't know if I really believed any more. Then one day I picked up my Bible, and do you know where it fell open?"

"The story of the virtuous woman," Skye responded, disappointed.

Charlie shook her head vehemently, laughter in her voice. "Not at all! It opened at James 1:5. *But if any of you lacks wisdom, let him ask of God, who gives to all generously and without reproach, and it will be given to him.* Of course, I'd asked God for guidance before, but this time, I bared my heart. I desperately needed to hear from Him, because I was questioning my ability and commitment to being a mother and a wife. I guess it was fairly normal, but I think in hindsight I was suffering from post-partum blues, and I felt my life was imploding."

"Wow. I had no idea," Skye said.

"No, not many people did. It's not something easily shared with others, especially when your husband is in a leadership position."

"So, what happened?"

"After I bared my soul, I knew deep inside that I would be okay. The next day I was offered a job as a kindergarten teacher that I'd applied for months before I even had Teya. I didn't have to leave her to go to work, and I immediately felt I had my identity back."

She smiled, met Skye's gaze. "Sometimes we just need to hold on and sit tight through the times when we feel completely lost. God will see to it that something shifts, eventually. Not all who wander are lost. Even Jesus went out into the wilderness."

Skye hugged Charlie, but although her words had offered hope, Skye's mood hadn't truly lifted until this morning's service when she'd felt the presence of God in her heart. If only she could worship like that every day.

As they sat under the trees, she gazed out over the landscape. Charlie's words had been apt. This was a wilderness, in a way. Certainly a desert. Yet, in spite of that, she *was* finding joy here as well as toil. She smiled at Noufou's two small daughters as they ran up to her, waved and ran away again, laughing. Femke admonished them with a smile.

"What are their names?" Skye asked.

Femke replied in broken English. "These two, Liana and Nanci. My boys over there helping prepare food, they are called Issa and Ismael. They are good boys."

"She thinks so," Noufou said good-naturedly. "I think they're all rascals! Especially this one." Grabbing Liana, he tickled her and was rewarded with shrieks of delight.

Skye leaned against the acacia trunk and watched them, grateful to have been invited into their group. She glanced at Scott, who was staring into the distance beside her. She tapped his thigh when Ismael placed dishes of potatoes and rice on a shawl on the ground in front of them, his face beaming.

Although she was wrestling with the heat and the hard work, Skye loved being here. Being amongst these beautiful, humble people made moments like these so precious.

Charlie approached with a jug held high, her own face glowing. "We have lemonade!"

The children squealed as they all lined up for Charlie to fill their cups.

"I guess water shortages can be a real threat this time of year," Skye said to Noufou as she sipped her bottled water.

Noufou nodded, a grim look on his face. "Yes. A drought can put the whole community into...crisis?"

Skye nodded to confirm his choice of word before he continued. "But perhaps worse is dirty water. Then it brings disease, and we have no real doctors here."

"No doctor?

"No, we have to go to the city for medicines too. Often we have to wait a long time, or pay, but they are too expensive for most of us here."

Skye wondered if a mission to provide health care wasn't just as urgent as building houses. As a nurse, she couldn't imagine the horror and chaos of an infectious disease and no access to the medicine needed to treat it. They took so much for granted back home.

After lunch, she strolled back to the mission house with Scott rather than returning in the van with the others, glad of the chance to spend some time with him. "What did you think of the service?" she asked as she linked her arm through his.

"It was...different." He paused. She was about to ask him to elaborate when he continued. "Do you know what those words on the wall mean?"

"*Jehovah Shammah* and *El Shaddai*?" she asked.

"I think that was them."

"I only know because Dad has a book on old Hebrew names for God. *Jehovah Shammah* is from Ezekiel. It means 'God is there' or 'God is here', depending on the context. *El Shaddai* is more obscure, but it refers to God as our sustainer, blesser and nourisher. It's interesting because it can also mean 'many-breasted one', which refers to God's mothering of us. It's amazing isn't it? We put God in boxes. But really, God is so much more than we can ever imagine. He's everything. He's even a mother."

Scott looked at her pensively. Growing up without a mother, she sensed he often longed for a mother's caring hug, although he never said. He shook his head. "You know so much."

"Not really, but it's not just about knowing things, it's about feeling them."

He sighed heavily. "You felt it in there, at the church, didn't you?"

Skye nodded. "Didn't you?" she asked gently.

Scott was quiet for a while, then he answered almost flippantly. "Yeah, a bit. I'm not sure about all that dancing around, though."

Skye chuckled, but secretly she thought that letting go and doing a bit of dancing would do Scott a world of good. Maybe next time. She squeezed his arm and prayed silently for him.

10

The days passed with a familiar rhythm. Skye grew accustomed to the work and made fewer mistakes, earning praise from the team for her resilience, but her restlessness and discontent persisted, however much she tried her best to overcome them. The sun continued to burn down and she looked forward to cooler nights sitting on the verandah with the team and her friends, and snatched moments alone with Scott.

Scott also settled into the repetition of their days and thought less about what he'd left behind. He deliberately tried not to think about the future and what he would return to. His company seemed another world away, let alone another country. He looked forward to getting out onto the site each morning, and took a fierce pride in the houses they were creating.

He was even making friends. After the first Burkinabe church service, he'd surprised himself by striking up a tentative friendship with Noufou. Similar in build and strength, they often found themselves working as a pair. Even so, Scott was conscious of keeping a little distance. After all, they'd leave when the three months were up and would never see these people again. He'd hesitated when Noufou invited him and Skye to dinner at his house in the village. Skye, of course, said yes instantly, and seeing the delight in Noufou's eyes, Scott could hardly begrudge her acceptance. Still, he wondered what to expect a few days later as he and she made their way to Noufou and Femke's house.

If you could call it that. Scott tried his best to keep his face blank as they entered Noufou's home to a warm welcome from Femke and the children, but as he glanced around the basic structure, his thoughts turned to his modern and stylish apartment back home. No matter how long he was here, he would never get used to the standard of living in the village.

"You have a lovely home," Skye said to Femke with complete sincerity. Not for the first time, Scott wished he could see the world a little more as she saw it. Femke thanked her shyly and returned to the kitchen area, which was so basic he wondered how she managed to prepare any meals at all. Skye followed her, chatting away, and he stood with Noufou outside in what he supposed was the garden, although it was more of a mini farm with chickens, a goat and even a small pig, all scrummaging around. The heat intensified the pungent aroma of the animals, and Scott fought the urge to gag.

He'd been in the village long enough to know that while Noufou may seem incredibly poor to him, by the standards of the village people, his family were among the more comfortable. Noufou showed him the animals proudly and Scott did his best to look impressed. After all, he thought wryly, he didn't have animals in *his* back yard and wouldn't have a clue about how to look after them if he did.

"We're using this morning's eggs for dinner," Noufou said proudly, nodding at the chickens.

"Sounds great," Scott said with complete honesty. He didn't think he'd ever seen a freshly laid egg, let alone eaten one. Suddenly he was quite looking forward to what he'd expected would be a meagre dinner. They didn't have chickens at the mission house, so it had been weeks since they'd enjoyed an egg.

Skye came outside, her face downcast. "Femke won't let me help," she explained.

Noufou nodded. "No. You are a guest," he said, as if that settled the matter. Scott knew hospitality was important in this place, and he felt surprisingly humbled that Noufou had invited them, given that they clearly had barely enough to sustain themselves.

Scott met Skye's gaze and smiled sympathetically as she slipped her hand into his. He squeezed her hand but returned his attention to Noufou. "Will the boys follow you into building?" he asked.

"Issa, I hope. He is good with his hands. Ismael, he likes his learning. He hopes to go to the city and study. They are good boys." Noufou's face shone with pride when he talked about his children.

"What do you do? At home?" Noufou asked, and Scott realised he'd talked to the team very little about himself since being here. He started to tell Noufou about his work and his promotion, then stopped. What would all of his successes mean to a man like Noufou? Suddenly, Scott felt ashamed of the urge to brag. "I'm an engineer," he answered simply. He caught Skye's gaze, and felt his face grow warm at her widened eyes followed by a smile of approval.

Nanci ran into the yard, tugged at Skye's shorts, and babbled something in French through a gap-toothed smile. Skye laughed and picked the little girl up.

———

"DINNER IS READY," Femke announced from the doorway and waved them into the house. They found places around the wooden table next to the cooking area while she laid the table with greens, grains and a dish that looked like scrambled eggs. It smelled divine. They sat on low, rough wooden benches rather than chairs. The children clambered onto one, jostling each other for room until a sharp look from Noufou quieted them.

Femke was the last to sit, again refusing all offers of help from Skye. Although he clearly adored his wife, Noufou made no offer of help. Skye got the impression that he simply took it for granted that cooking and serving were Femke's jobs. There was a more traditional division of labour here, she knew, and she was coming to understand that women in general were accorded less status than men, a thought that made her bristle. There were some things about home that she definitely preferred, she thought as she watched Femke anxiously bustling around and tending to the children, barely touching her own food.

The meal was delicious, and Skye told her so. Femke blushed and looked down shyly, reminding her of Scott in the garden, deliberately downplaying his achievements to Noufou. She was proud of him. She'd expected him to launch into a litany of all his successes and had been virtually cringing in anticipation of it. Instead, he'd displayed a humility she'd never seen in him before coming to Burkina. The place was changing him, just like Charlie had said it would.

Just how it was changing her, other than raising uncomfortable feelings, Skye wasn't sure. But she pushed those to the back of her mind and tried to concentrate on enjoying Femke and Noufou's company. Little Nanci had taken quite the shine to her and kept trying to climb onto her lap. She seemed fascinated with Skye's hair, reaching out to touch it. Her parents reprimanded her but Skye waved them away, laughing. The little girl and her siblings were adorable with their dark hair and skin, and eyes that shone every time they laughed or smiled. Skye couldn't help but wonder what it would be like to have children of her own. With Scott. She shot him a quick glance and a mixture of emotions swirled in her heart. They'd never talked about it, though, even in a general way, and she had no idea if children fitted into his plans for the future. Still, she supposed they were young enough that it wasn't a priority just yet. And right now, she had no idea what the future held for them as a couple, anyway.

"Will you have children?" Noufou asked as if reading her thoughts, looking from her to Scott. Skye glanced at Scott and cringed with embarrassment when he coughed.

"Er...yes, I suppose. One day," he said without looking at Skye. She wondered if Noufou assumed they were married or at least engaged, and realised the couple was only ten years older than her and Scott at most. They would have gotten married and had their first child while still in their teens.

Scott avoided her gaze after that. After they thanked Noufou and his family for a lovely evening and left on a round of hugs, particularly from little Nanci, they began to stroll back to the mission house in awkward silence.

Taking the bull by the horns, Skye broke the silence first. "You looked shocked when Noufou asked about children," she said.

Scott shrugged helplessly. "I didn't know what to say...I know lifestyles are very different here. I guess it's expected to have children."

"Don't you want to have kids one day?" She felt a crushing disappointment that was only slightly lifted when he shrugged again.

"Probably, yeah. Not for a while, though. There's so much I want to achieve first." He frowned, no doubt thinking about his lost promotion.

"I noticed you downplayed what you do to Noufou," she said gently, setting aside her disappointment.

Scott gazed ahead as they walked and took a moment to answer. She could hear the sincerity in his words as he spoke. "It just seemed pointless, going on about promotions and projects. It would mean nothing to him, and..." His voice trailed away as he brushed a fly from his face. "That made me wonder if it means anything at all."

Compassion filled Skye. He was clearly calling his life into question in a lot of ways and it couldn't be easy for him. She took his hand and squeezed it. "I'm glad you're starting to see things differently, but it's still okay to be proud of yourself. You've achieved so much."

"Thanks," he said with a touch of his usual confidence, but then he grew serious again. "I'm starting to wonder what it's all been for."

Skye stopped and gazed into his eyes. Eyes that she'd come to love, that melted her heart every time she looked into them. He met her gaze, but his discomfort at their emotional intimacy was evident. Why had she never seen before just how wounded he was? Underneath that arrogant exterior, a lost little boy looked back at her.

"There's a purpose for everything, Scott. God can use and transform anything. I think it's good that you're questioning your priorities, but that doesn't mean everything you've done so far means nothing. Maybe it's just leading you in a different direction than you realised. I'm really proud of how far you've come."

He blinked, and his mouth twitched. She wasn't used to seeing his guard down. "You mean it, don't you?" he said softly. "I don't think anyone has ever believed in me the way you do."

Skye's heart broke for him, and she had to resist flinging her arms around him in the middle of the street.

"God does," she said simply.

He blinked and shook his head, almost as if he didn't believe it. If only he knew how much God truly loved him. They carried on walking, and she gripped his hand tighter. She enjoyed the sensation of his fingers curling around hers and the warmth of skin on skin. It felt so right when they were together like this.

Scott's words cut in to her moment of contentment. "How are you, Skye? You seem a little...I don't know, withdrawn? Playing with Nanci today was the happiest I've seen you in days, apart from at church."

They'd gone to the local church again on the weekend, and

once again he'd resisted joining in the more active worship, although Skye had seen his foot tapping. "I'm okay," she said, not wanting to go into her conflicted feelings. Scott frowned. "Don't give me that. What's wrong, Skye?"

She sighed. "I truly don't know," she said honestly. "I just feel sort of flat, yet restless at the same time. I thought I'd love it here, and I do, but I don't feel that I'm doing the right thing." She shook her head, exasperated that she couldn't find the words for how she felt.

"Not doing the right thing? You were so dead set on coming here. Do you want to go home?"

"No," she replied truthfully. "Being on mission has been a dream of mine for so long and I still believe in that. We're clearly doing good here. We're not just building houses. People like Noufou are learning a trade they can pass on. It's a great project. I just feel out of place." She shrugged. "Maybe it's because I'm finding the work so hard. I'm not good at it, I'm not keeping up, and I don't feel I'm contributing anything of real value." Her voice faltered as she verbalised thoughts she'd been holding tight since they arrived.

"That's not true," Scott said softly. "You're doing great on site. I know you struggled at first, but you've really got into a rhythm now."

She blinked back tears. "I guess I don't find mud bricks that interesting." Drawing a steadying breath, she forced a brighter tone. "However, I've never seen you more engrossed." Skye smiled.

He grinned. "It's crazy, isn't it? This work is the last thing I saw myself doing, but I'm really enjoying it. And you're right—it's going to make a big difference. I couldn't believe Noufou and Femke's house. It looked like it could fall down at any minute."

She nodded. He was right. The new houses would make life for the local people better in so many ways.

They were just a few streets away from the mission house.

Skye hoped the others would be out or in their rooms so she and Scott could have some time together in the garden alone. They hadn't talked like this for a long time. If ever.

"Have you talked to Charlie about how you feel?" he asked.

She sighed. "Yes. She was really helpful, but I think it's something I've got to get through myself. I'll keep praying about it."

Scott looked thoughtful. "Praying really works for you, doesn't it?"

"Yes, but it's not a magic trick." She laughed lightly and then grew serious. "Prayer's just communicating with God, being honest, seeking what *He* wants. Being pliable in His hands. But some things are a process, and there might not be any immediate answers." She paused, drew a deep breath. "I think this challenge is one of them. I'm not going to pretend I'm not frustrated. I've always felt so sure of what God wanted for me and where I'm going in life. To be so unsure feels like the ground shifting under me."

Scott let go of her hand and pulled her in for a hug, dropping a kiss on the top of her head. She leaned in to the warmth and comfort of his arms and sighed happily. Being held felt so nice after all their restraint since being here. She relaxed, enjoying the brief respite from her inner turmoil.

"It'll be okay, Skye," he assured her. "You'll work it out. And we're not here forever."

Skye nodded, although she didn't want to tell him she felt just as ambivalent at the thought of going home. They arrived at the mission house and went straight out onto the verandah. She was relieved to see they were indeed alone. They sat on the makeshift decking next to each other, staring out across the landscape. Its sparse beauty never failed to touch her, to remind her of the diversity and wonder of Creation. She took Scott's hand again.

He turned to face her, his expression serious. Bubbles of perspiration dotted his forehead. "I'm glad we've got some time together, Skye." His voice was soft, like his eyes. Her stomach fizzed. It had been too long since they'd kissed properly, and it had been her fault. He lifted his hand and stroked her cheek gently. "I've been thinking about our future a lot lately. Even before we got here."

"Oh?" Her heart beat a little faster.

Scott cleared his throat. "Yes. I've never been serious about a girl, until you." He paused, gazed deeply into her eyes. "You mean the world to me, Skye."

"I feel the same," she whispered.

He lowered his face towards her. She tipped her lips to meet his. He paused, his mouth so close she could feel his breath. Her heart pounded in anticipation.

"Skye, I..."

Loud male voices approached from the hall.

Scott groaned and raised his head.

"Hey, guys. How was dinner?" John and Tim appeared on the verandah, completely oblivious to the moment they'd interrupted.

Skye caught the expression on Scott's distressed face and stifled a giggle.

————

SCOTT SLUMPED onto his bed and held his head in his hands. He'd begun to warm to his team mates over the last few weeks, but it would be quite easy to cheerfully bang John and Tim's heads together. It had been the perfect moment to propose to Skye, and he'd seen the expression in her beautiful eyes. She would have said yes, he was sure of it.

As he balled his fists, feeling sorry for himself, a phrase Craig had quoted often popped into his head. 'In God's time, not ours'. Scott sighed and raised his head. There'd be another chance. Even so, he couldn't help hoping that God's time wouldn't turn out to be too different from his own.

His gaze fell on his still unopened Bible at the side of his bunk. The evening sunlight streaming through the window played across the cover. Dust particles danced in the light—a reminder of its lack of use. He picked it up, feeling the weight of it in his hand, and allowed it to fall open on his lap. Nervous anticipation filled his gut.

The page fell open at a passage in Matthew he'd heard spoken about in church but had never taken any heed of. When he began reading, it was as if he was seeing it with fresh eyes.

When Jesus saw His ministry drawing huge crowds, He climbed a hillside. Those who were apprenticed to Him, the committed, climbed with Him. Arriving at a quiet place, He sat down and taught His climbing companions. This is what He said:

'You're blessed when you're at the end of your rope. With less of you there is more of God and His rule.

'You're blessed when you feel you've lost what is most dear to you. Only then can you be embraced by the One most dear to you.

'You're blessed when you're content with just who you are—no more, no less. That's the moment you find yourselves proud owners of everything that can't be bought.' [The Message]

The words spoke directly to him, and Scott felt a stirring inside. For hadn't he, in a sense, lost the job and the status that had meant so much to him and had become part of his identity? And yet he suddenly could see, as though a veil had dropped from his eyes. In making the pursuit of success so important, he'd prevented himself from drawing near to God. A God who didn't sound at all like the punishing patriarch his father had spoken of —who was of course a reflection of *his* father himself—but a God who wanted to embrace him. Hold him. Scott swallowed hard as deep sadness welled inside him and he remembered himself as a little boy, desperate for his father's love, longing to be embraced without judgment, but was denied. When tears dropped onto the page and he realised they were his own, he grabbed a tissue and wiped his eyes and the page before continuing.

The next line, too, seemed to have been written for him. When had he ever been content to be who he was, without striving for more? His whole adult life had been about striving for more and having more because ultimately, he felt that he needed to *be* more. He'd never felt good enough, and yet, here was the Lord telling him he *was* good enough just as he was, right here and now. A desperate longing to believe that truth welled inside him.

He read on, his hands shaking as he smoothed the page, now damp from his tears.

'You're blessed when you've worked up a good appetite for God. He's food and drink in the best meal you'll ever eat.

'You're blessed when you care. At the moment of being 'care-full,' you find yourselves cared for.

'You're blessed when you get your inside world—your mind and heart—put right. Then you can see God in the outside world.

'You're blessed when you can show people how to cooperate instead of compete or fight. That's when you discover who you really are, and your place in God's family.'

The words were a gentle rebuke. His workplace had always been about competition, even during team projects, and his whole life had felt like a fight. And when had he ever really shown care for anyone, other than Skye?

This was not the Bible he remembered from his youth or his father's angry sermons. This was a whole different perspective on life and faith. How had he not known? How had he sat in church all these years and never truly heard or understood this most simple and yet so revelatory of messages? He felt overwhelmed in a way he couldn't describe. An energy moved through him that he couldn't name, that seemed to fill every cell, every pore, every hidden and secret place, revealed and transformed. There was no shame, only healing.

He knew what Skye would name this feeling.

The Holy Spirit.

He read on, amazed by the beauty and simplicity of the verses. At how Jesus explained justice and love in ways that would have been radical at the time—and were still radical in practice now, but at the same time were so simple. So true. Forgiveness, faithfulness, and the exhortation to be true to one's self and to God. It all made perfect sense.

The last lines of the Sermon on the Mount were like a hammer between the eyes.

'In a word, what I'm saying is, 'Grow up'. You're kingdom subjects. Now live like it. Live out your God-created identity. Live generously and graciously toward others, the way God lives towards you.'

Scott fell to his knees. Tears streamed down his cheeks as a wave of warmth flowed through him, and he knew he was seeing himself as God saw him. Not as a weak, useless child, like his father did, but as a precious and much-loved son. "Lord God, thank You for loving me. I don't know how to, but please help me to grow up, to become the person You created me to be. I've been so self-focused, and I'm so sorry. Please mold and shape me. I'm willing to live Your way."

He remained on his knees and did business with God for the first time in his life. Finally, he understood what Skye and Craig had been telling him—that God loved him just the way he was.

Afterwards, he lay on his bunk, eyes closed, a little unsure what had just happened to him. His rational mind tried to reason his experience away, but Scott knew that something had changed deep inside in him. Something had been awakened.

It was a beginning.

11

One morning several days later, Noufou didn't turn up for work. Expecting him to eventually appear or send someone with a message, the team got on with the task at hand. As the end of the work day approached, however, when there was still no word, they began to feel a sense of unease.

Yacouba said he'd check on Noufou on his way home, and the rest of the team returned to the mission house as usual. Skye couldn't shake off a sense of foreboding, no matter how hard she tried to reassure herself that Noufou's absence was most likely nothing.

They were eating dinner when Yacouba appeared at the door and called Craig and Philip outside. Skye and Scott exchanged a worried look across the table. When Craig returned, his face had grown white. He took Charlie and Teya outside and was gone for several minutes. When he came back, he asked Paul's team to gather on the verandah.

They all followed him out silently. Skye prayed fervently that nothing had happened to Noufou, although she sensed her prayers were in vain.

Outside, Craig swallowed hard. Skye had never seen him

look so concerned. He cleared his throat and took a deep breath. "One of Noufou's children has fallen ill. They thought it was nothing at first, but little Nanci took a turn for the worse this afternoon, and now another of the children and one of his neighbour's has fallen ill." He paused. Steadied himself. "They think it's typhoid."

Paul sucked in a breath and Skye felt a surge of panic. "How bad is it?" she asked, thinking of Noufou and his family, and of little Nanci who days ago had been climbing all over her.

Craig ran his hand over his hair and directed his response to her. "Out here, with little access to medication? It can be devastating. It's especially dangerous for children. As you'd most likely know, typhoid starts a bit like the flu, often with a rash, and can then cause severe intestinal problems—even a hemorrhage."

Skye clutched Scott's arm, her head spinning. She'd learned about typhoid but had never had any direct experience with it. "Can it be cured?" she asked quietly, trying to remember what she'd been taught.

Craig deferred to Philip, who shrugged. "It's treatable with antibiotics, although some strains are becoming resistant. The challenge here is getting hold of the medication we need. We need to get a doctor here as fast as we can."

Craig nodded. "I'm going to let everyone know what's happening, but I wanted to tell you guys first since I know some of you are close to Noufou and his family. Yacouba is already on his way to the city to get a doctor. Charlie and Teya have gone with him. They'll stay there until we know what's happening." The fear in his voice was evident. He didn't need to add *until it's safe to return*... Skye leaned against Scott. He rubbed her arms gently. John and Tim stood silently, but their anxiety was clearly etched on their faces.

"Is it contagious?" Tim finally asked.

Craig nodded again. "We'll all be at risk, so it's important we do our best to contain it. Philip will go over everything with us.

The children and the elderly are our main concern at the moment, being the most vulnerable."

As they went back inside the mission house, Skye reached for Scott's hand. She wished she knew what to do or how to help. She was a nurse after all. She couldn't sit around idly while people were ill.

Once the news had been announced, the discussion focused on what they should do. When Philip said they'd set up a sick area for anyone affected in the village, Skye offered her help immediately. "I'm a nurse," she said. "Well, in my final year."

Craig and Philip nodded gratefully.

"I'm definitely not a nurse," Scott said, surprising her, "but anything I can do to help, I'm there."

"Thanks." Craig gave Scott a firm nod.

Skye was surprised at Scott's offer, but perhaps not as much as she would have been once. This past week she'd noticed a definite change in him. He seemed calmer, more at peace, and he'd even danced a little at church with an expression of real joy on his face that had warmed her heart.

There'd be no dancing for a while now, though, she thought glumly. She prayed again that the sickness would turn out to not be typhoid after all, and the children would recover quickly. In her gut, though, and despite her prayers, she sensed the foreboding she'd experienced earlier in the day would most likely be proved true.

THE NEXT DAY, the children had worsened. Skye thought her heart would break when Noufou and Femke arrived at the makeshift sick tent the mission group had set up, with a semiconscious Nanci and Issa in their arms. Femke turned haunted eyes to her, but was unable to speak. All Skye could do was clasp the woman's hands and tell her they'd be praying, and that a doctor was on the way. She hoped it was true.

By the afternoon, more sick people, predominantly children, had arrived at the tent. Skye took charge quickly, organising into groups those who'd offered to help with some taking care of clean bedding, some boiling water, and others sitting with the sick. Without medicine, there was little else they could do except keep the tent as sanitary as possible and keep the patients hydrated and clean. Nevertheless, the smell of sickness swept through the tent.

"How can I help?" Scott had asked earlier that day, his eyes large and pleading. She realised he'd probably never seen sickness of this magnitude before. She'd sent him to do an inventory of what stock they had—blankets, utensils, antiseptics etc. Supplies turned out to be pitiful, and she felt exasperated. Why hadn't anyone at the mission project thought to prepare for such an eventuality? Surely health was more important than building houses? But as the day turned into evening and more and more sick people streamed in, she barely had time to think about anything but assisting however she could.

Scott insisted she go back to the mission house to get some sleep, but she refused.

"You need to sleep," he said in worried frustration. "Other people are here, and there's little anyone can do until the doctor arrives."

"*If* he arrives," she said, her reply tinged with exhaustion. There'd been no word from Yacouba. "I want to stay, Scott, but you go. I've worked nights and days at the hospital back home before. I'll be fine."

"I'm staying with you," he said in a tone that brooked no argument. Even so, Skye opened her mouth to protest, but when he smiled at someone behind her, she turned around and smiled, too. Yacouba had returned.

Her smile quickly faded. He was alone. "Where's the doctor?" she whispered loudly, trying to mask the desperation in her tone.

Yacouba shook his head wearily. "No one can come yet. They

said they'll send someone as quick as they can. In the next few days." He shrugged, as if not surprised.

Skye buried her head in her hands, trying not to panic. There were so many sick people, and they all needed medicine, and she was running out of supplies. "I need a minute," she said to both men. She rushed out of the tent and stared up at the night sky imploringly. She felt like screaming, but instead, she called out to God. "I don't know what to do, Lord. Please help us. We need a doctor." She dropped to her knees, the gravity of the situation weighing heavily on her heart, soul and body.

Sensing someone standing over her, she looked up. Scott crouched next to her and placed his hand on her shoulder. They stared at the stars in silence for a few moments before he spoke. "I've been praying a lot lately, but I guess it's times like this that prayer is really needed," he said quietly.

Skye nodded. His words warmed her heart. She was glad he'd been praying but she was too tired and worried to process properly. Everything felt surreal, caught in a single moment in time, and her focus was on the sick children and the fear of how much worse the epidemic could get.

"We need a miracle, or a doctor," she said somberly. Back home, they took health care for granted. If she was sick and needed a doctor, she'd be in and out of a medical centre within a few hours, the prescribed medicine in hand. Even in the event of serious illness, a hospital and trained medical staff were never far away. Here in Teganega, all they had was a tent, some blankets, and her, a nurse who was not fully trained. Why wasn't the government doing more to help these people? Why wasn't the West doing more? God had provided enough resources in the world to go around, and yet there was this searing inequality. Something that had always been an abstract concern was now completely up close and personal, and Skye wanted to scream at the unfairness of it all.

When a scream split the air, she thought for a moment it had indeed come from her, but when Scott jumped to his feet, she did the same, and they both sprinted back to the tent. In the far corner, a mother cried over a convulsing child. Skye ran to her side, took the child from her arms, and shouted for help and water. At the same, she tried to clear the young girl's airways. As the girl went limp and still in her arms, the mother began to moan low in her throat. Skye tried desperately to resuscitate the girl, all her training coming to the fore, even as she knew it was hopeless.

She laid the girl down, a wave of hopelessness breaking over her. "I'm so sorry," she said to the mother. A wail that would haunt her forever rose from the woman as she gathered her daughter into her arms, sobbing and rocking the tiny, lifeless body. Skye turned away. Tears streamed down her face, and she was only barely aware of Scott pulling her to her feet and of other helpers rushing to comfort the mother and remove the child from her arms, since the infection risk was great.

Skye stumbled as she walked out of the tent with Scott. Only when they were far enough away that the others wouldn't hear, she fell into his arms, sobbing. He held her, caressed her. When she pulled back, there were tears in his eyes. "I should have been able to save her," she whispered.

Scott shook his head. "No, Skye," he said firmly. "You did everything you could."

"It wasn't enough," she cried. When he tried to respond, she cut him off, shaking her fist in the direction of the tent to make him understand. "Not just me, this. All of this. It's not enough. We can't treat typhoid and we won't be able to contain it. They'll die, Scott. Noufou and Femke's children will die." She broke down again, and this time Scott pulled her to him without speaking as she sobbed into his chest.

A SHORT WHILE LATER, Skye agreed to return to the mission house to get a few hours sleep. Before she left, she changed her clothes in the sanitary area they'd set up and placed her dirty clothes into boiling water. They had to pray that supplies of clean water didn't run out.

She walked with Scott to the mission house in silence. He didn't know what to say.

Philip met them at the door. He was on his way out, and he too, looked exhausted. "We're holding a prayer vigil at the church to pray for the sick."

"Pray for a miracle," Skye said wearily, going inside.

Scott answered the question in Philip's eyes. "A little girl just died," he explained, "and Yacouba came back with no doctor. It could be days before anyone arrives, and more and more people are getting sick."

Philip sucked in a deep breath. "Then it's a miracle we'll pray for," he said. He searched Scott's eyes. "How are you? Have you been with Skye at the tent all night?"

Scott nodded. "I wish there was more I could do. I feel so helpless."

Philip's face softened. "You're doing plenty. God sees it all. He sees your heart." He squeezed Scott's shoulder as he stepped past.

Scott pondered those words as he went inside to find Skye. If God truly saw his heart, what would He see? He'd been trying to follow through on his promise to live God's way, but felt he wasn't doing too well in the faith and trust department.

Seated at the dinner table, Skye appeared deep in thought. "You need to get some sleep." He stood behind her and massaged her shoulders.

"I don't know if I'll ever get that mother's face out of my mind," she answered, her voice breaking. Scott slipped onto the seat beside her and put his arm around her shoulder, drawing her close.

"I doubt I will either."

12

Arriving at the tent the next morning, Scott and Skye discovered that three more people had died in the night—two children and an elderly man. Skye accepted the news with a grim nod and got to work straight away. Scott was assigned to the laundry, washing bedding that became filthy again as soon as it was cleaned. Despite the unrelenting work and the urgency of the situation, the repetition soothed him. At least he was doing something useful in the face of such hopelessness.

The girl's death yesterday had affected him more than he'd expected. Like Skye, he doubted he'd ever forget the raw grief displayed by the child's mother. An increased air of fear hovered over the tent since the deaths had started occurring. If there'd been any lingering hope that this would not turn out to be typhoid, to not be life-threatening, it had been dashed once people started dying.

Scott had never been up close with either grief or sickness before, tending to avoid people who were ill. Just a few months ago he would have found this whole situation disgusting and would have fled from it as fast as humanly possible. His only concern would have been for himself and Skye. Now he desperately wanted to help, and he was deeply concerned for the villagers, especially for Noufou, who had become a friend. In spite of the cultural and lifestyle differences between them, Scott held a place in his heart for the proud, friendly Burkinabe man who had so little, yet had gladly shared what he had with them.

Stopping for a break, Scott approached Noufou who was sitting with Nanci, his face haunted. The little girl was mercifully asleep, but just one glance revealed all was not well. She was still running a fever and was covered in an angry rash. There had been little change in her condition since she'd been brought in yesterday, other than growing progressively weaker. Issa was showing signs of improving and had been moved to a connected smaller tent. Older and stronger than Nanci, his chance of recovery was greater.

When Scott sat, Noufou turned anguished eyes to him. "Where is the doctor?" he asked, his English more broken than usual, his grief apparent in his voice.

Scott could only shake his head. He didn't know. Craig had received word from Charlie that morning—she and Teya were fine and showing no symptoms. Charlie had been to the main hospital pleading the village's case, but had been given the same answer as Yacouba. As soon as a doctor and medicine were available, they would come. Two days at the most. Scott looked at Nanci and knew she didn't have that long. All they could do was pray.

He had been praying since that night in his room when the Word of God had become real to him, and even now, in the midst of tragedy, he knew something deep within him had changed. He hadn't spoken to Skye about it yet. It had been such a precious, life changing moment that he still hadn't processed fully, but he'd tell her soon. Until the illness had hit, his heart had felt lighter every day.

Now it felt as if it would break.

. . .

HE RETURNED TO THE WASHING, deep in thought. How had his emotions suddenly become so raw? Where had this deep concern and compassion for others come from? It was almost more than he could bear.

After several more hours, a girl from the mission house relieved him. Grateful for the respite, Scott went into the tent to look for Skye. She was deep in conversation with Maria, who'd volunteered to help today, since more people had turned up in need of care. Instead of intruding, he decided to go to the church to join those who were praying. He washed and changed carefully, hoping it was enough to reduce the spread of any infection, and made his way to the church.

The scene that greeted him was very different from that of the last few Sundays. No dancing or musical instruments. Instead, candles flickered on a makeshift altar, and a group of people gathered round, sitting or kneeling, murmuring prayers. Wary of spreading infection, Scott remained at the back and sat on one of the rough benches. He bowed his head and added his prayers to those of the villagers.

He thought of Noufou, of the desolation in his friend's face as he helplessly watched his daughter sicken, and in spite of the horror of the situation, Scott also thought about the force of the love the man had for his child. Just like the gutteral wailing of the mother yesterday, born out of a broken heart. Was this what it was like to truly love? He thought of the possibility of losing Skye, and an icy hand clamped around his heart. No wonder people like his father, like himself, became so closed to any real emotion, when this was the pain it left you vulnerable to.

And yet, Scott knew he would not, *could not*, go back to that closed off place. For all of the pain he was witnessing and experiencing, a part of him longed to be loved the way those parents loved their children.

He sensed someone standing over him and looked up. *Skye.*

She looked exhausted, with dark circles under her eyes and a grey hue to her tanned skin.

"How are things at the tent?" he asked, even as he could read the answer in her expression.

She shook her head, her gaze fixed on the glow from the candles as she sat beside him. "We lost another one," she said in an expressionless tone, as if all emotion had been wrung out of her. "An eleven-year-old boy."

He didn't know what to say. Platitudes were pointless. Instead, he took her hand gently in his. They sat in silence for several moments before he asked how Nanci was.

"The same."

"That's good, isn't it?"

Skye rubbed a hand across her face. "Well, it's better than her getting worse, but she's so small. I don't know how much longer she can hold out with that fever raging through her. Femke has resigned herself to losing her. I don't know how to give them hope when I feel like I'm losing it myself."

There was nothing to say. They sat together for a long time, both lost in their prayers, their hopes and their fears. Both trusting they would be heard.

———

THE NEXT MORNING, Skye steeled herself as she made her way into the sick tent. She'd been so tired, that despite all the worry, she fell into a deep sleep and woke to the sun streaming through the window onto her face. For a moment she'd felt peaceful and ready for the day, then the remembrance of what was happening flooded in on her. Anguish and heartache replaced her peace.

She hurriedly dressed and headed to the tent. Although all the children needed care, she couldn't help her gaze going straight to Nanci. Noufou sat in much the same position she'd left him the night before. She wondered if he'd even moved. She went over and pressed her hand to Nanci's forehead.

"She feels cooler," she said, hope lifting in her chest.

Noufou opened his mouth to say something, then his eyes went wide at something behind her. "The doctor!"

Her heart beat wildly as Skye turned to see that there was, indeed, a Burkinabe doctor making his way through the tent. He carried a large bag that she prayed contained the medicine they needed.

"Who's in charge here?" the man asked a worker, who pointed towards Skye. *When had that happened?* She certainly didn't feel in control of anything, but hurried towards the doctor, who had crouched down next to a young boy and was examining him, while asking questions of the mother in native tongue. Skye waited while he examined a few more children before he addressed her, his expression serious.

"It's typhoid," he confirmed in English.

She bit her lip. "I thought so. Did you bring medicine?"

"Yes. I should have enough antibiotics to administer to everyone who is sick, but I have to be honest. They may not work."

Skye's heart sank like a stone into her stomach. "Not work?"

The doctor shook his head sharply. "Some strains of the disease are becoming resistant. All we can do is hope. If this doesn't work..." His sentence trailed off, but there was no need to finish it. They both knew the dire consequences of the medicine being ineffective. The infection would spread, and more villagers would die.

Skye and the others got to work preparing patients. Thankfully, the doctor had brought more supplies with him also, including antiseptic swabs. She tried her best to focus on the job at hand and not on the expressions of hope in the parents' faces. Each time an antibiotic was administered, she offered up a desperate prayer that it would work. When Noufou lifted Nanci in his arms, she fought back tears.

The doctor left to visit the village, for not all those who were sick had been able to make it to the tent, especially the elderly. Skye kept herself busy cleaning and ensuring all the patients had fresh water to drink, all the while watching for signs of improvement.

Returning to the sick tent later that afternoon, the doctor administered the next dose of medicine. "I'll be back in the morning," he told Skye. "We'll know by then if the antibiotics are working, though for some of the children it may be too late."

After he left, Skye checked on all the patients again before handing them over to Maria who had volunteered to do the night shift. Stepping outside the tent, she sucked in the cooler night air, pausing to look up at the stars. Although she knew that God was everywhere, gazing at His amazing creation usually brought her closer to Him. She offered a prayer of thanksgiving before continuing on.

Scott had already left, having been at the tent early that morning, even before she arrived, and he had worked solidly all day. The change in him both amazed and pleased her.

There'd also been a change in her.

The anger and frustration she'd felt the day before still remained, and had, in fact, grown. That these people were left without proper health care and housing and an adequate supply of medicine while so many people like herself took those things for granted made her sick. It was, she was sure, the very opposite of the justice and all-encompassing love that her faith demanded. She could no longer simply stand by and do nothing, not now that her eyes had been opened. Something had to be done.

Growing up, Skye had always wanted to be a nurse. Right from the start when she was young, she played hospital with her dolls and had never doubted that nursing was God's calling for her life. After the last few days, in spite of how awful the situation was, her resolve had only strengthened. She was certainly a lot better at nursing than she was at building houses.

It had never before occurred to her to be a nurse anywhere other than Australia. It was her home, with plenty of sick and needy people. Yet now she was beginning to wonder if her skills wouldn't be better put to use elsewhere, like here. If the antibiotics worked—and she knew it was a big if—the epidemic had still revealed the desperate need for health care for the residents of Teganega. Although there was only so much she could do alone, ideas started forming in her head as she walked through the village to the mission house.

Diseases like typhoid were often exacerbated and spread by poor hygiene and lack of simple sanitary supplies. If they set up even a basic clinic, where she could give out supplies to families and teach people basic ways to help keep infection at bay, over time, that could make a real difference. It wouldn't even cost a great deal, certainly not compared to the cost of the building project. The more she thought about it, the more determined she became. She'd speak to Craig and Philip about her ideas as soon as possible. And she wouldn't take no for an answer.

Having a purpose made Skye feel stronger in the face of the hopelessness that had threatened to engulf her over the last few days. She thanked God for showing her a way forward, whatever tomorrow might bring.

13

The next morning, Scott had once again arrived at the sick tent before Skye. When she walked inside, he was sitting with Noufou and Nanci. He called her over.

She hurried to the group holding her breath, ready to face the worst, because Noufou was cradling his daughter in his arms. Skye's heart hammered in her chest. She prayed that didn't mean...

But the sight that greeted her brought tears to her eyes. Little Nanci was half sitting in her father's arms, her eyes open. She still looked weak and ill but was clearly lucid, and she even managed a small smile for Skye.

"Oh, thank God," Skye murmured as she crouched down and examined the little girl. Pleased that her temperature had fallen and that the medicine was clearly working, she smiled at Noufou. "She's going to be all right. But she needs to eat, even though she might not manage much. Take her to the back of the tent and Ellie will get her some food."

Noufou nodded gratefully. Before he made his way to the back, he grasped one of Skye's hands and met her gaze. "Thank you." He spoke with such sincerity that tears once again sprang to her eyes.

She turned to see Scott looking at her with pride. "I didn't do anything," she reminded him. "The doctor is the one we should thank."

"No, you did so much, Skye. You kept them going, kept everyone as safe as you possibly could until he got here."

She tried to smile, but the thought of all the children they'd lost weighed heavily on her. She thought again of her plans for a clinic and resolved to speak to Craig that afternoon.

With Noufou and Nanci being looked after, Skye did the rounds of the tent, checking on the other patients. Overjoyed that the majority were already improving, and some were even sitting up and playing, she thought her heart would burst with happiness. For some patients, however, it was still touch and go.

The doctor came again as promised with another round of antibiotics. Skye had heard that Craig and Charlie had personally provided some of the funds for the medicine. The mission paid for the rest from their meagre resources.

The doctor was pleased that the children were responding, and like Scott, he heaped praise on Skye for all the work she'd done.

Again she shrugged it off, mentioning the rest of the team, determined not to take credit for something she had only been a part of, albeit an integral one.

Once all the patients had been attended to, she walked back to the mission house with Scott. When she explained her idea for a clinic, he responded enthusiastically. "I think it's a fantastic plan." He smiled at her. "I'm sure Craig and Philip will go for it. When will you talk to them about it?"

"Now," Skye said as they entered the dining room at the mission house.

Seated at a table, Craig looked up and waved them over. "I

hear things are improving," he said eagerly. His eyes were bloodshot and puffy, as if he hadn't been sleeping either.

"Yes, praise God," Skye responded, her pulse quickening. *Was it the right time to speak to him?* She took a deep breath. There was no time like the present. "Craig, can we have a quick chat before dinner? I've got some ideas I'd like to discuss in light of the typhoid crisis."

He angled his head, looked slightly puzzled, but agreed immediately. As he led her to a small meeting room, Scott winked and gave her a thumbs up.

She smiled as their gazes connected. The change in Scott was truly amazing. It was hard to believe he was the same person who'd resisted coming on mission, but she was so glad he'd come.

Taking a seat opposite Craig, her pulse raced again. Not just from nerves, but from a real sense that this idea was God ordained, and that He was with her, batting for her.

Craig leaned forward and gave her a weary but genuine smile. "Before you tell me your ideas, I just want to say how grateful we all are for the work you've done over at the tent. You handled this crisis amazingly well, Skye. I honestly don't know what the villagers would have done without you."

"Thank you," she said humbly. Although the praise and acknowledgment meant something to her, it paled in comparison to the sheer relief she felt that the situation was improving, and her urgency to prevent it from happening again.

"It couldn't have been easy, especially with the supplies incredibly low," Craig continued.

Skye leaned forward in her chair, eager to put her ideas across. "Yes, and that's what I wanted to talk to you about. I know it's impossible to predict these things, but we can go some way towards prevention with basic health care and hygiene. It's not the whole answer, however. What's needed is a properly funded health care system and affordable access to medicine, but changing the government's priorities takes time." She paused and inhaled another deep breath. "I've been thinking a real and immediate difference can be made if we set up some kind of health care clinic in the village." She'd said it, put it out there. Now it was up to him.

Craig scratched his head. "How would it work?"

Skye shifted in her seat. "Well, I could run a drop-in clinic and also do talks on basic hygiene, boiling water, ways to prevent infection spreading, and so forth. We'd need a translator from the village. I was thinking of Femke. I could also teach some of the women to run classes themselves and so it could be a real community thing. Much like the building project." She was talking too much, too fast, but she couldn't contain her enthusiasm.

Craig nodded, his eyes brightening. "I think it's a great idea. Charlie said we needed something like that here, but the immediate need has always been for housing. But now that this crisis has taken place...you're right, it could have been prevented."

Excitement welled within her. Her plan was coming together. Well. Not her plan, per se. It had to be God's plan, because it felt so right. Not only could she actually be of real use here at last, but a health clinic could have far-reaching benefits for the community she'd come to cherish for a long time after she went home.

Thinking of going home gave her another idea. "Maybe I could train some of the mission leaders in basic hygiene, too. I could put some worksheets together. That way there'd be information to pass on, because the mission may not always have volunteers with any clinical training. There are so many possibilities. I don't want to get ahead of myself, but I can really see a project like this working here." *And I don't want it to fall by the wayside after I've left...* This wasn't just about her proving her usefulness. It was bigger than her and so needed to be sustainable.

Craig drummed his fingers on the table, thinking. "We'll need to get the board's approval. Philip will support it, but the challenge will be in convincing the trustees. We'll need funds."

"Like I said," Skye countered, "a project like this could help prevent further outbreaks. We had to use precious funds to get the antibiotics, right? A clinic is going to prove a lot cheaper in the long run."

"You're right. And it's a shame it's taken such a crisis for action to be taken. Leave it with me. I'll speak to Philip and we'll get the ball rolling with the board. If we're successful, we could have you set up within a week or so."

Skye shook his hand. "That's wonderful. Thank you."

They had less than two months left before going home but it would be long enough to make a difference, to get the project started. After the hopelessness that had swamped her in the face of the typhoid disaster, which of course wasn't yet over, she could see a small way forward.

"Shall we pray?" Craig asked.

"That's a great idea. Should I grab Scott?"

"Absolutely," Craig said, then added, "I've noticed a change in him, even before this happened."

Skye nodded. "He hasn't said anything, and I don't want to push him, but yes, you're right. I think God's been at work in him."

"I'm so pleased," Craig said, smiling warmly.

"As am I."

Skye practically ran to get Scott, energised by purpose. Finding him in the dining room where she'd left him, she gave him a quick summary of her conversation with Craig, and he readily agreed to join them for prayer.

Seated opposite Craig, Skye took Scott's hand as Craig led them in prayer for the new project. A deep sense of gratitude welled inside her as he prayed.

"Lord God, thank You for Your love, and for the lessons You've taught us by being here amongst the people of Teganega. And yet, we can't help but be saddened by the loss of life and touched deeply by the grief of family members, but thank You for the opportunity to bring change and hope to the people of this village that this will never happen again.

"Thank You for Skye and her love and commitment to the people here. And thank You for her skills. Lord, please guide and lead us in this new venture, and we also ask that the board will approve and support it. But Lord, most of all, we ask that You comfort those families who've lost loved ones, let them rest in the knowledge that they're now safe in Your arms, and that one day they'll be reunited."

Pain squeezed Skye's heart at the mention of those who'd died and were now with Jesus, but then she remembered little Nanci, and appreciation swept the pain away.

After Craig finished, she opened her eyes and glanced at Scott. He stared at her with an expression she could only describe as love. Her heart felt as if it could explode. Blushing, she squeezed his hand and lowered her gaze.

Later, after dinner, Craig led the team in a short thanksgiving service, also attended by a number of villagers. The antibiotics were making a real difference. An elderly man had passed away, already too weakened by age and sickness for the medicine to help, but all the children were responding well. Skye volunteered to do another night shift at the tent, figuring she could sleep the next day. Scott offered to join her.

As they worked, he kept glancing at her, an expression in his eyes she couldn't quite read. The crisis had brought them closer. She'd seen a softer, more caring side to him that she'd always hoped was there but until now had been hidden, and he'd seen and comforted her at her most vulnerable. She sensed this was a turning point for them both.

14

By the end of the week, all those who had been sick with typhoid had improved sufficiently to return to their homes, and life in the village slowly returned to normal. The board approved Skye's plan to run a drop-in clinic. The makeshift sick tent was thoroughly cleaned and disinfected and transformed into a place where the locals could come to learn better hygiene and also have their minor health issues cared for. Skye had at last found her peace and purpose, and each day she thanked God for His provision.

The houses came along nicely, and the day that Noufou and Femke and several other families moved into their new ones was a day of celebration. The whole village came together to mark the occasion, which commenced with a thanksgiving service at the church. Once more, the chapel was filled with singing and dancing, and the joy of the Lord rang out as they praised God for His goodness and mercy.

Scott smiled at Skye as they worshipped together. Since the typhoid crisis, they'd grown so much closer and had spent many hours talking about issues that truly mattered. He'd told her about the night his eyes had been opened as he read the Bible, and since then, he'd been hungry to learn more. It was like a veil had been lifted from his eyes and his heart had expanded. Everything he'd heard before was now meaningful and relevant.

They often studied the Bible together in the evenings. Sometimes it was just the two of them, sometimes others joined them. Having shared such an intense experience together, when death had reared its ugly head and stared them in the face, everyone in the team had become more aware and appreciative of the precious gift of life they'd been given, and were eager and willing to allow God to mold and shape their hearts and lives. Including Scott.

Skye returned his smile, and when the singing stopped and they sat, he took her hand and laced his fingers with hers. He couldn't think of anywhere he'd rather be right now than here in this remote village with the love of his life. The need to propose had lessened, although he occasionally thought of the beautiful ring tucked away amongst his belongings. When the time was right, he'd ask her to marry him. He no longer needed her to wear his ring to be sure of her love. He saw it in her eyes every day. Felt it in her voice. He still longed for the day when he could truly love her as her husband, but he would wait. In God's time. Not his.

Later, after the service finished, he and Skye and several others helped Noufou and Femke move into their new home. It was an easy move, because they had so little, but the joy on the children's faces as they stepped inside the house for the first time brought a lump to Scott's throat. The family would be happy there, and even though it was still a basic house by western standards, it was their home, and it would be blessed with the love of God and of the parents for their children. Little else was truly needed when all was said and done.

Scott met Skye's gaze and they shared a smile as Noufou gathered his family and the team members together to pray God's blessing on the home. He prayed in his native tongue. It didn't matter. His heartfelt prayer, full of gratitude and humility, transcended language barriers.

Walking back to the mission house much later, Scott suggested they detour by the lake. Skye readily agreed. The sun was low in the sky, and the heat of the day had started to dissipate. He slipped his arm around her shoulder and pulled her close as they walked together. They had one week left before returning to Australia, but he was in no hurry to leave.

"Did you ever think that all of this would happen when you invited me to come?" he asked.

She shook her head and chuckled. "I had no idea about anything. It was just a big adventure, and I was so naïve. But I'm so glad we came. It's been such a wonderful experience, and I know that I'll be going home a different person."

"As will I. I was so blind to everything before. This has changed my life. Thank you for asking me. For believing in me."

He dropped a kiss on the side of her head and pulled her tighter as they walked on.

Reaching the lake, they sat on the ground. Waterbirds skimmed the surface searching for food. Some nested in dead tree branches which created a silhouette against the orange sky. It was a beautiful setting. Scott felt his heart quicken. He didn't have the ring with him, but it didn't matter. He lifted his hand and ran the tip of his finger down Skye's hair line, turning her face gently towards his. She met his gaze. He tried to throttle the dizzying current racing through him as his heart beat faster.

Her lips lifted in a coy smile. "What are you up to, Mr. Anderson?"

He ran his fingers through her hair. "I'm just thinking how special this moment is. How many men get the chance to sit in such an amazing place with such a beautiful woman?"

She laughed, but then grew serious as his gaze intensified.

He gulped. "Skye, this trip has changed my life. I never expected it to. In fact, I only came because of you."

"Well, I'm glad you came."

"So am I. My job back home seems so irrelevant now. The promotion, the pressure to perform, to impress." He shrugged. "They all seem meaningless now."

"They're not. You know that. It's just that your priorities have changed."

"Yes, they definitely have. And other than God, you're my number one priority." He swallowed hard. "Before we came, I thought I loved you, but I realise now that it was a selfish love. Nothing like the love I've seen in action here, and that I now have for you. We've come so far, and I love you with all my heart. I want to spend the rest of my life with you, to support and encourage you. To have children with you."

Her eyes widened, but when she started to speak, he placed his finger over her lips. "I'm asking you to marry me, Skye. Will you have me as your husband?"

Her face lit up in the widest smile he'd ever seen before she threw her arms around his neck. "Yes, yes and yes," she shouted as she kissed the side of his head.

He pulled her back and met her gaze. Her eyes shone and he felt his heart would burst. "I love you so much."

"And I love you, Scott. I can't wait to marry you."

Burying his hands in her hair, he pulled her face gently towards his and lowered his mouth. Her breath was warm and moist against his face, and his body tingled as their lips met. He moved his mouth over hers, devouring its softness. He could have kissed her forever, but the squawk of a bird interrupted the moment. He released her and smiled. "I love you, Skye. I promise I'll be a good husband."

"I have no doubt you'll be the best."

Skye's confidence in him warmed his heart no end. To love and to be loved was such a blessing. To share his life with her was a dream come true. Nothing would keep them from the adventure ahead or chase them back to the lives they'd been living before coming to this amazing place. They might return to Australia and to their jobs, but they'd take with them all the memories and experiences they'd shared amongst these wonderful people. People who had so little, yet so much. Who were blessed with love, and truly needed nothing else. Housing and health care improved their quality of living but didn't change who they were. Generous, loving people who found joy and happiness in the simplest of things. It was a lesson he was so glad he'd learned.

"Come on, we'd better head back. They'll wonder where we are," he said, jumping to his feet. He held his hand out and helped her up.

As she stood in front of him, he pulled her close and encircled her with his arms. She buried her head against his chest and leaned into him. As he kissed the top of her head, he gazed out at the fading sunset and silently thanked God for pursuing him like a long lost, but much loved son, for not giving up on him, and for offering him not only the gift of eternal life, but a life full of love and blessings in the here and now. With Skye. He pulled her tight and began humming the hymn they'd sung at the service that morning. His heart welled with gratitude at all that God had done, especially when Skye joined him.

To God be the glory, great things He hath done; So loved He the world that He gave us His Son, Who yielded His life an atonement for sin, And opened the life gate that all may go in.

Praise the Lord, praise the Lord, Let the earth hear His voice! Praise the Lord, praise the Lord, Let the people rejoice! O come to the Father, through Jesus the Son, And give Him the glory, great things He hath done.

They strolled back to the mission house together arm in arm. When they arrived, relieved that no one seemed to be around, he asked her to wait on the verandah.

She frowned. "What for?"

"Wait and see." He stole a quick kiss and then slipped inside.

Flicking on the light switch in the hallway, he shook his head and laughed when it didn't work. He didn't need it, because he knew where he was going and exactly where the ring was. In the semi-dark, he pulled his suitcase from under his bed and opened it. He felt for the box in the top zipped pocket. For a fleeting second, he thought it wasn't there. He began to panic but breathed a sigh of relief when his hand touched it. He pulled it out, removed the fancy wrapping, and opened it. The diamond glittered. It was a beautiful ring. He hoped Skye would like it. Closing the box, he slipped it into his pocket, zipped the suitcase up and placed it back under the bed before heading back to her.

He paused as he reached the door and took a deep breath. Would he have bought a different ring if he was buying it now? Months ago, he'd chosen it for show. But now, he realised with a smile, he would have chosen it for love. Blowing out his breath, he stepped onto the verandah.

Skye was leaning against the railing with her back to him. He studied her outline against the darkening sky and love for her filled him anew. To have her accept his proposal, here, in this most special of places, had been worth waiting for. Stepping quietly onto the verandah, he walked towards her, slipped his arms around her waist and nuzzled her neck.

She turned around slowly to face him. "So, where did you go?"

"Miss impatience!" He laughed, and then steadied his gaze on her. "I've had this with me since we arrived here. I've been waiting for the right moment." He reached into his pocket and pulled out the box.

Her gaze travelled from him to the box and back to him. "Wha..."

He put his finger to her lips. "Shhh..."

She giggled, but when he opened the box, she let out a small shriek. "Scott! I don't believe it. This is amazing. It's beautiful."

Smiling, he removed the ring from the box and slipped it slowly onto her finger. "A beautiful ring for a beautiful girl."

"I still can't believe it," she said as she examined the ring in the dim light. Slipping her arms around his neck, she stretched up to kiss him. "Thank you. I love it." Her breath was warm on his face, and he had a burning desire, an aching need, to kiss her passionately. But this was neither the place nor the time, so instead, he kissed her tenderly and gently.

"I'm so glad," he whispered in between kisses.

Laughing voices approaching the house interrupted their moment of intimacy. He reluctantly pulled away but looked deep into her eyes. "If you'd rather not wear it here, I'll completely understand."

She kept her gaze steady. "I know this would have cost more than Noufou can earn in a lifetime. The discrepancy between our lives and his seems so unfair, but you know, I think he and Femke will be happy for us. I'll be proud to wear it. But thank you for being so considerate."

He smiled. "You're welcome. I wasn't as thoughtful and understanding before we came here."

She laughed, tapping his nose with her finger. "I know."

The voices came nearer, and within moments, Tim, Richard, John, Ellie and Maria appeared on the verandah. Richard spoke first. "We wondered where you two had gotten to."

"They obviously wanted to be alone," Maria said, her gaze shifting to Skye's left hand. "What is *that*? Let me look." She stepped forward and grabbed Skye's hand, her face lighting up. "Really? You're engaged?"

Skye nodded eagerly, and Maria and Ellie threw their arms around her and then around Scott. Richard, Tim and John then shook hands with Scott and hugged Skye as they each offered their congratulations.

"This is cause for celebration," Tim said. "I'll get some drinks."

"I'll come with you," Maria said.

As they left, Scott caught Skye's amused gaze. They'd both wondered if those two might get together.

The pair returned soon after with some bottles of pop and packets of crisps. "It was all we could find, so it will have to do," Maria said as she opened the packets and offered them around.

"It's perfect," Skye said. "Thank you."

"So, here's to Scott and Skye," Tim said seriously. "May God bless you both, and mate, I just want to say, it's about time! That girl has been waiting to marry you since the day we arrived."

Scott turned and looked at Skye, his head tilted. "Have you?"

She shrugged, but the coy expression on her face and the way she clutched her hands in front of her answered his question in full.

15

As Skye had predicted, everyone, including the villagers, welcomed the news of their engagement news with excitement, and they all loved her ring. Charlie, in particular, was overjoyed, as was Femke. The team and the villagers organised a celebratory feast which also became a farewell gathering.

The forty houses that the team had been commissioned to build were finished and each had proud, new owners. Noufou, Yacouba, and the other Burkinabe apprentice masons were qualified and experienced enough to continue the work on their own, and to pass their skills on to other young men.

Skye was handing over the running of the clinic to Karen, Philip's wife. Femke, to Skye's delight, had agreed to be Karen's assistant. It truly was a cause for celebration, which started, as most things did in Teganega, with a church service.

After half an hour of joyous worship, the entire team was invited to the front and were prayed over and blessed by the pastor and the local people they'd grown so close to. A special blessing was prayed on Skye and Scott.

Skye clung to him for support as tears leaked from the corners of her eyes. She would miss these people so much, especially Femke and little Nanci, who'd almost claimed her as a second mother. It was a surreal moment. The intense heat, the noise of the musical instruments, the joyful worship and exuberant dancing, coupled with the heartfelt prayers of such beautiful, Godly people, was almost too much to bear. Standing there with Scott, her fiancé, made it even more surreal.

She wasn't the only one in tears. Maria and Ellie also dabbed their eyes with tissues. Scott handed her another when she began rummaging in her pockets. She gave him a smile of thanks.

They remained at the front with arms linked to sing the final hymn, which the team sang in English and the locals sang in their own dialect. It didn't matter. The heartfelt singing of *Amazing Grace* would please God no matter the language.

And then followed the feast, and what a feast it was. Partly prepared by the locals and partly by the mission, each dish had been lovingly made. Skye knew Scott was looking forward to eating steak once they got home, but he'd come to enjoy the basic food they'd been eating for the past three months, and she wondered what he'd prefer when they returned home. Home... her thoughts had been turning there more of late. Would she be happy returning to a normal, western lifestyle after experiencing all that they had in this remote place? It had been hard, and they'd faced plenty of challenges, but there'd been something exhilarating about living in this remote village that had changed her, and Scott, forever. Time would tell. In the meantime, she'd enjoy the celebration and the company of these beautiful people for one last day.

The celebration lasted well into the evening. The villagers knew how to enjoy themselves, and the time passed too quickly. Once all the singing, dancing, and eating were over, small groups gathered to chat around open fires as darkness fell. No one was in a hurry to leave. Skye and Scott sat with Noufou and Femke, who asked them more about their life in Australia. "Maybe you can come and visit one day," Skye said before she realised it would be highly unlikely they could ever afford to do so.

But Femke replied that she'd love to. "One day when the Lord sees fit, we will come."

Tears sprang to Skye's eyes. "And you will always be welcome. You and the children." And she meant it. She had no idea what they would think of the decadence of her first world nation if they came, but that was no reason for them not to visit. She had no doubt that neither Femke nor Noufou would be envious of the lifestyle that so often placed possessions above people. They were happy with who they were. Comfortable in their own skins. What they owned was secondary. Their family was everything to them. The challenge for her and Scott when they returned to their homes and families was to remember and emulate the generosity of the people in Teganega who had so little.

The evening drew to a close, and after hugs all round, she and Scott wandered back to the mission house with the others for the last time. The following day, they were leaving for a five-day tour before heading back to Australia.

Their bags were already packed, and so, instead of going to bed, most of them stayed outside and talked all night until the first rays of daylight appeared over the vast savannah, giving promise of another brilliant new day. Skye leaned into Scott and hummed worship songs, her heart welling with praise and gratitude for all the blessings God had given them.

"Hey, time for bed." He kissed the side of her head.

She nodded. A few hours of sleep would be good before they headed off. He helped her up and walked with her to their rooms. They shared a hug before going their separate ways. As she slid onto her bunk for the last time, Skye smiled sleepily at Maria and Ellie who had also just come in, before her eyelids closed.

SEVERAL HOURS LATER, Skye was woken by Charlie who had taken on the role of getting everyone up in time for when the bus arrived. She groaned but crawled out of the bunk and dressed in khaki shorts and the white t-shirt she'd kept out of her bag. The other girls also dragged themselves out of bed and dressed. "We shouldn't have stayed up so late," Maria said, yawning.

Ellie laughed. "You were having too good a time with Tim."

Maria blushed. Skye had certainly noticed how close the two had become, and it warmed her heart. She hoped that they would find as much joy and happiness as she and Scott had found.

Once dressed, the girls checked the room to make sure nothing was left behind, and then wheeled their bags out to the main area. Scott and the other males were already gathered and were chatting in a group. Skye's heart jolted when he turned and their gazes connected. She loved the beard he'd been cultivating while they'd been here. It made him even more handsome.

Soon, the bus arrived and they were saying their goodbyes. Philip and Karen assured them they'd be welcome back at any time. Noufou and Femke and the children came to see them off. Tears spilled down Skye's cheeks when she hugged Femke, but her heart broke when little Nanci held her arms out. Skye picked her up and hugged her. "I love you, Nanci. Be a good girl for your mummy." Her words caught in her throat. She kissed the little girl and then passed her back to Femke before she broke down.

The rest of the villagers waved as the bus drove slowly through the village and headed towards the open road. The driver stopped the bus at the new houses on the edge of the village so they could take photos, and then they off for five days of exploring this country. Several months earlier, it had just been a dot on a map, but now it held a special place in all their hearts. Burkina Faso, 'land of the upright people'.

During the five days they toured the country, they saw the rugged outcrops of the Sindou Peaks, explored the national parks, and marvelled at the abundant wildlife at Lake Tengrela.

They stayed in guesthouses run by families who made them feel welcome, and although the capital city of Ouagadougou, commonly called Ouaga, lacked impressive architecture and parks, they enjoyed the vibrancy of the city which was a hive of performing arts. Dance, live music, and craft markets abounded.

And then it was time to board the plane and commence the long trip back home to Australia.

16

Three Months Later

SCOTT SAT AT HIS DESK, staring blankly at his computer screen. *Another mega shopping mall.* How many shopping malls did one city need? He ran his hands over his hair and leaned back in his chair. Since returning from the mission trip, he'd struggled to settle back into his job. Mike had welcomed him with open arms and hinted that the promotion might still happen. Scott read between the lines...Derek wasn't performing. That didn't surprise him. What did surprise him, however, was that he didn't want the promotion.

He didn't want to spend all his time behind a computer screen, working extended hours on extravagant constructions while all he could think of were the mud brick houses he'd help build. Once, he would have considered the offer of a promotion a boost to his ego, but now, his identity came from being a loved child of God. He didn't need prestige and promotions to make him feel good.

He sighed and got to work. For now, this was his job, and he needed to work at it as if working for the Lord, and he needed to be grateful he had a job. Glancing at the photo of Skye beside his desk, taken at the front of the mission house in Teganega, he smiled. He couldn't wait to marry her.

When they arrived back in Sydney, they'd immediately driven to her parents' place. He should have done the right thing and asked for her father's approval before proposing, but it was too late. He'd already proposed, and she'd already accepted, so it had just been a matter of announcing their news. Fortunately, both her father and mother had been delighted, and now, the wedding date was approaching. The week after she graduated as a nurse, they'd become husband and wife. His mood suddenly buoyed. He would suffer anything for Skye. That included designing a shopping mall he thought now was a complete misuse of money.

At the end of the work day, Scott wished his colleagues, including Derek, a happy evening, and hurried downstairs to meet her. They were having a pre-marriage counselling session with Craig that evening but were meeting for a quick dinner beforehand.

He smiled when she waved to him from across the busy road where she stood with a crowd of other people at the traffic lights, waiting for them to change. His heart fluttered at the sight of her. When the lights changed, she stepped onto the road and walked with the throng towards him. But then, the unthinkable happened. A car ran the red light and barrelled into the pedestrians, knocking them flying. Scott's heart stopped. Pandemonium broke out. People scurried all round, yelling for help. He had eyes for only one person. Skye.

She'd been dragged along the road and now lay several metres to his right. Her body was lifeless. Still. Fear splintered his heart as he sprinted to her. She had to be alive. This couldn't happen. Not now. Not after all they'd been through. He reached her. Bent over.

Someone else crouched beside him. "She doesn't look good,"

the man said, lifting her wrist to feel for a pulse. Scott stared at her, feeling numb. She had to be alive. She had to make it. He gripped her other hand. Stroked it. "Come on, Skye. Wake up. Please." He looked at her chest, hoping to see it rise and fall.

"She's got a pulse. It's weak, but it's there," the man said.

Hope rose inside him. "Call an ambulance, somebody," he yelled at no one in particular.

"It's on its way, mate," the man said. "Can you hear it?"

Scott listened. The man was right A wail of sirens sounded in the distance and grew louder by the second. All round, people hovered, trying to get a look at the tragic scene. The car that hit the pedestrians had stopped and the young driver was already being interviewed by police. He'd been restrained and appeared agitated. Scott wondered if he was on drugs.

At a glance, Scott counted five others who'd been injured. One was covered with a jacket. He gulped and prayed for that person and their family. It could have so easily been Skye.

His heart soared when her eyes flickered and then opened. "Thank God!" He pressed her hand to his lips.

A number of ambulances arrived and one stopped near them. Two paramedics jumped out and hurried towards them. Scott and the man moved aside to let them take over. The man and woman knew what they were doing, and after a making a quick assessment and asking Scott if Skye had been unconscious at all, said they'd take her to the hospital to be fully checked, but they believed she would be okay. Tears sprang to Scott's eyes. "Can I go with her? I'm her fiancé."

"Sure. Come with us," the woman said.

Scott held Skye's hand as she was wheeled to the ambulance.

"Can you call Mum?" she asked. "And Craig."

He nodded, relieved that nothing was wrong with her cognitive functions. He prayed she had no internal injuries. "I'll call them now."

Soon after arriving at the hospital, while Scott waited for the doctors to examine Skye, her parents arrived. John and Maryanne Matthews had become like second parents since he and Skye announced their engagement, and his heart went out to them. He recalled the grief of the Burkinabe mother when her tiny child had died of typhoid, and the selfless love of Noufou as he sat vigil beside little Nanci day and night while she hovered between life and death. John and Maryanne held the same kind of love for Skye. He could see it in their eyes as they approached him. Although he'd assured them she was okay, they rushed over and asked how she was doing and if they could see her.

Scott knew little more than when he'd called them. "We just have to wait," he told them.

"I can't believe this has happened," Maryanne weeped. Of medium build and with the same colouring as Skye, she was an attractive woman who was showing little signs of aging, although Scott guessed she was nearing fifty. His own mother would have turned fifty this year if she'd lived. But he'd never known her. She'd died giving birth to him, which was possibly one of the reasons his father had treated him so badly, although he'd never said so. Scott wondered if his father blamed him for his mother's death.

He gave Maryanne a hug. "I know. Neither can I. One minute she was walking across the road, the next, she was lying on it."

"Well, at least you were there for her."

"Yes. At least there's that."

They were about to sit when a doctor poked his head into the waiting room and called them over. They quickly crossed the room and stood in front of him. He addressed John and Maryanne. "You're the parents?"

John extended his hand. "Yes. John Matthews. And this is my wife, Maryanne."

The doctor took his hand and shook it. "Nice to meet you. I'm Dr. Potocki. I've already met Scott." He nodded Scott's way. "Well, I've got good news. Your daughter is very lucky. No internal injuries, just a lot of bruising and grazing. We'll keep her in for observation overnight since she was unconscious, but she should be right to go home tomorrow."

Maryanne began to sob. John slipped his arm around her shoulder. "I'm sorry," she said. "I can't help it. I'm so relieved."

"It's perfectly understandable. It could have been a whole lot worse," the young doctor said.

"Can we see her?" John asked.

"Sure. Follow me."

Scott stepped aside and allowed Skye's parents to go ahead of him. She was in a small cubicle, half-sitting, half-lying on the bed. A number of pillows had been tucked behind her head. She smiled when they entered, and after quickly catching Scott's gaze, she turned her attention to her parents, holding her hand out to her mother. "I'm sorry."

"Oh, don't be silly, darling. You've got nothing to be sorry for. It wasn't your fault."

"I should have paid more attention."

"You were crossing on a green light. The driver was in the wrong, not you."

"I heard that someone died." Skye's eyes flickered.

"Yes. An elderly woman. It's so sad," her mother replied. "But we're so glad you're okay, darling." She squeezed Skye's hand. "And that Scott was there for you."

Skye smiled and shifted her gaze to him. "Yes, my knight in shining armour."

He laughed. "Not really. You were only there to meet me."

She chuckled, immediately wincing and clutching her side. "I shouldn't laugh."

"Sorry." He sobered. "How bad does it hurt?"

"On a scale of one to ten?"

He nodded.

"Eight."

"My poor darling." Maryanne's voice faltered.

"I'll be all right. I've just had some pain medication. I'm sure it'll kick in soon."

"I hope so," her mother said. "Is there anything we can get for you?"

Skye shrugged. "I didn't plan on spending tonight in the hospital."

"I can grab whatever you need," Scott offered. He tapped Maryanne's arm lightly. "Stay with her. I'll be back soon. I'll just grab what I think."

"You don't have a car here," Skye pointed out.

Scott chuckled. She was right. There was definitely nothing wrong with her mind.

"Take mine," her father offered.

Scott blinked. His own father would never have let him take his car, even now. "Thanks. That's great." He accepted the keys and kissed Skye's forehead. "I'll be back soon. Anything in particular you want?"

"A change of clothes. Toothbrush. Bible. But you'd better take my keys as well." A smug smile flitted across her lips.

"Right." He glanced around for her purse, and then realised he'd picked it up off the road and still had it looped over his shoulder. He acted so flustered, anyone would think it had been him who'd been hit, not her. He handed it to her so she could find her keys, which she did.

"Fleur might be home, but I'm not sure."

"Okay. I'll be back soon." He squeezed her hand and then left.

Climbing into her parents' car, he reached for calm before starting the engine. Once more, the thin line between life and death had reared its head. He couldn't bear to think about losing Skye, but praise God, she was relatively unharmed. Not that long ago, he'd shied away from getting close to people out of fear of being hurt, but he was starting to understand that it was that very vulnerability that drew people closer to each other and to God. And he now knew that God, being loving and kind, would sustain him through whatever life tossed at him. He didn't need to live in fear and isolation any longer.

When he reached Skye's house, her roommate wasn't home, so he quickly found the things Skye had asked for and packed them into a small bag. As he was leaving her room, a card on her desk caught his attention. Not normally one to read other people's personal mail, he almost ignored it, but something drew him to it. He hesitated, but then picked it up. It was a card from her parents...

Dearest Skye,

We can't tell you how happy we are that you've found true love with Scott. He's such a fine young man, and we know he'll be a wonderful husband and provider. Your dad and I are so proud of you, and we know that you and Scott will have a blessed future together, wherever God leads you.

As much as we'd love you to stay close, we know your heart is elsewhere, so all we can say is that you should follow where God leads. We'll always love you and will be there for you whenever you need us.

We so look forward to what God is going to do in both your lives, and we pray Paul's prayer that he prayed for the Ephesians for you:

"For this reason, I kneel before the Father, from whom every family in heaven and on earth derives its name. I pray that out of His glorious riches, He may strengthen you with power through his Spirit in your inner being, so that Christ may dwell in your hearts through faith. And I pray that you, being rooted and established in love, may have power, together with all the Lord's holy people, to grasp how wide and long and high and deep is the love of Christ, and to know this love that surpasses knowledge—that you may be filled to the measure of all the fullness of God."

With much love and blessing,

Mum and Dad

Scott sat on Skye's chair and brushed tears from his eyes. To know that her parents believed in him was almost more than he could bear. If only his own father felt the same way. It hadn't been his fault that his mother died. Well, not directly. But it seemed he'd borne the blame for it all his life. But Scott knew he had to let it go. He had no control over his father's thoughts and attitudes. That was between him and God. He, himself, had been given a new start, and he was grasping it with both hands. He was like the clay that Craig had talked about on the first morning at Teganega. His heart was open and pliable, and as a result, God was molding and shaping him into what He wanted him to be. It helped that he had Skye to spur him on and encourage him.

Before he left to return to the hospital, he bowed his head in prayer. "Dear Heavenly Father, I feel so blessed to be part of this family, to be loved and accepted by them so completely. Thank You for them, and thank You for being there for Skye this afternoon, and that she's not badly injured.

"And I'm so grateful to You for making me part of Your family. I'm sorry it took me so long to understand what You're all about, so thank You for being patient with me and for believing in me. And on that note, I pray for my dad. Lord, I know he blames me for my mother's death, but I pray that he'll one day surrender his bitterness to You. In the meantime, Lord, please help me have a good attitude towards him. To show him Your love, and to not let his harsh words affect me.

"Thank You, Lord. In Jesus' precious name. Amen."

Scott rose, replaced the card onto Skye's desk, and then stepped outside before driving back to the hospital. Although he felt guilty about reading her private card, it also gave him added respect for his future in-laws, and so, when he returned the keys to Skye's father, he held his gaze a little longer than he normally would have. In John Matthews' eyes, he saw a man who cared deeply. A man he could emulate as he became a husband, and one day, God willing, a father. Scott smiled and thanked him.

"You're more than welcome, son."

Scott could hardly contain the tears that lay just below the surface.

17

The day of Skye and Scott's wedding finally arrived. They'd agreed on a simple ceremony and reception. After being in Teganega, neither wanted a lavish affair. In fact, if they could have held it in the village, they would have been more than happy, but instead, they opted to have the ceremony beside a lake that reminded them, in part, of the reservoir. Only this lake was surrounded by lush, green grass, and instead of a view across the savannah, they had a view of hazy mountains. But the views didn't matter. Soon after they made their vows and became husband and wife, they'd be returning to Africa.

The night of Skye's accident, they'd had a long discussion in her hospital room about what they truly wanted to do and where they felt God was leading them to live and serve. Africa had gotten into both their hearts, and after praying about it, they decided to apply to a number of mission agencies. Several had been interested, but they were thrilled to be accepted by Shalom Christian Mission, where they would be heading to South Sudan after doing some intensive training and preparation. Once again, Scott had to look the country up, since he'd only ever heard of it in passing and knew little about it. Only slightly less poor than

Burkina Faso, the country faced many of the same issues: poverty, malnutrition, disease, and sub-standard housing. He and Skye would be working amongst some of the country's poorest people. Scott's boss, Mike Jennings, had once again thought Scott had lost his marbles, as did his father. But Skye's parents and their church community supported their decision and promised to not only pray for them, but to provide financial support.

Scott was standing under an arch of flowers thinking about their future when a murmur moved through the crowd. His head turned, and his heart lurched at the sight of her. In the simplest of wedding gowns, Skye looked stunning. As she walked towards him on her father's arm, his pulse raced when she flashed him a magnificent smile. That this beautiful woman was about to become his wife was a dream come true.

She finally reached him. Her father shook his hand and then placed Skye's hand in his. The ultimate confirmation that he was accepted. Not just accepted. Loved.

He met her gaze and smiled.

Craig Holloway cleared his throat and officially welcomed everyone. "Such a wonderful and special occasion. I've witnessed the blossoming love between these two under the most trying of situations, and I'm so pleased to officiate at their wedding. Will you all join me as we commit their union to the Lord?" He caught Scott's gaze and winked before bowing his head.

Scott ran his thumb gently over Skye's hand as Craig began his prayer. When she responded with a squeeze, a deep sense of peace filled him. This was the beginning of their life together as a married couple. Adventure awaited them, of that he was sure. But so did a lifetime filled with love and blessing.

Later, after they'd been pronounced husband and wife and he'd kissed her for the first time as her husband, Scott approached his father. He'd been shocked to see him there before the ceremony began, since he hadn't replied to the invitation. They'd exchanged a nod at that moment, but now, Scott felt compelled to speak with him. The few times they'd seen each other since he and Skye returned from Burkina Faso, Scott had hoped his father's opinion of him might be changing, although nothing he said suggested that. In fact, if anything, his words had grown more negative and biting. Scott truly had little idea of what went on in his father's head, but he knew that the man was filled with bitterness and regret, and that even though he professed to be a Christian, he certainly didn't live it out. Scott knew what it was like to have his eyes opened to the truth of the gospel message, and he knew how transforming the love of God was, and that no one, not even his father, was beyond His amazing, redeeming, love and grace.

"Dad." He extended his hand as he approached more confidently than he felt. Taking a deep breath, he smiled weakly, and then, instead of shaking his father's hand, he stepped closer and wrapped his arms around him. "I'm so glad you came." His voice hitched as he pushed the word from his lips.

His father seemed taken aback. He remained rigid, as if he didn't know how to respond. It was the first physical contact they'd experienced that Scott could remember, so he understood. But now, the ball was in his father's court. He'd taken a step to reconciliation, and in time, he prayed that Dan Anderson might forgive him for living, and they might be able to forge a healthy father-son relationship.

Scott released him and stepped back. It was an awkward moment, so he was grateful when Skye joined him. She held her hands out to his father. He took them, and he even kissed her cheek. Now, that didn't surprise Scott. No one, not even his father, could resist Skye's charm.

Skye's dad also joined them, and they left the two fathers to chat. Scott slipped his arm around her waist and stole a kiss while they walked towards the photographer. "Can't wait to get you alone," he whispered in her ear. A grin spread across his face.

She laughed and playfully punched his arm. "You might have to wait a little longer. The photographer wants us."

"I know," he said with resignation. "I guess I've waited this long. What's another few hours?"

"Exactly. And we have a lifetime to look forward to."

"Yes, we do. And I can't wait to start that life together."

AFTER A SHORT RECEPTION held on the lawn alongside the lake, Scott whisked Skye off to a small cottage in the mountains for their first night together. He'd arranged with the local restaurant to deliver a special dinner at seven p.m., giving him plenty of time alone with his new wife before it arrived.

Their wedding was filled with wonder and love, and neither wanted it to end. But when the sun rose the next morning, they drove back down the mountain and bid a tearful farewell to her parents and their close friends. They were honeymooning in the southern state of Victoria before heading to the city of Melbourne to embark on their training. They'd see their family and friends briefly before flying to Africa, but this was the start of their adventure.

While hugging and kissing everyone before Skye's father drove them to the airport, a real sense of blessing washed over Scott. God had changed his heart in so many ways. His priorities, thoughts, and attitudes had all changed. Skye had told him it was the Master Potter at work in his life, and he knew she was right.

But the fruit of the Spirit is love, joy, peace, forbearance, kindness, goodness, faithfulness, gentleness and self-control. Against such things there is no law. Galatians 5:22-23

NOTE FROM THE AUTHOR

I hope you enjoyed "Blessings of Love" and the way that God, the Master Potter, gently brought healing and wholeness to Scott and Skye's lives. You can check out the blog post about the story here (http://pottershousebooks.com/happy-release-day-blessings-of-love-by-juliette-duncan-is-now-available-to-read), and while you're on The Potter's House website, why not check out all of the other Potter's House books? Read them all and be encouraged and uplifted!

- Book 1: The Homecoming, by Juliette Duncan
- Book 2: When it Rains, by T.K. Chapin
- Book 3: Heart Unbroken, by Alexa Verde
- Book 4: Long Way Home, by Brenda S Anderson
- Book 5: Promises Renewed, By Mary Manners
- Book 6: A Vow Redeemed, by Kristen M. Fraser
- Book 7: Restoring Faith, by Marion Ueckermann
- Book 8: Unchained, by Juliette Duncan
- Book 9: Gracefully Broken, by T.K.Chapin
- Book 10: Heart Healed, by Alexa Verde
- Book 11: Place Called Home, by Brenda S Anderson
- Book 12: Tragedy & Trust, by Mary Manners
- Book 13: Heart Transformed, by Kristen M. Fraser
- Book 14: Recovering Hope, by Marion Ueckermann
- Books 15: Blessings of Love, by Juliette Duncan
- Book 16: Until Christmas, by T.K. Chapin
- Book 17: Heart Restored, by Alexa Verde
- Book 18: Home Another Way, by Brenda S. Anderson

- Book 19: Proven Love, by Mary Manners
- Book 20: Dawn of Mercy, by Kristen M. Fraser
- Book 21: Reclaiming Charity, by Marion Ueckermann

BE NOTIFIED of Juliette's new releases by joining Juliette's Readers' list http://www.julietteduncan.com/linkspage/282748, also receive a free thank-you copy of "Hank and Sarah - A Love Story", a clean love story with God at the center.

ENJOYED BLESSINGS OF LOVE? You can make a big difference. Help other people find this book by writing a review and telling them why you liked it. Honest reviews of my books help bring them to the attention of other readers just like yourself, and I'd be very grateful if you could spare just five minutes to leave a review (it can be as short as you like) on the book's Amazon page.

READ a bonus chapter of my newest book, "A Time to Treasure" below. Enjoy!

CHECK out all of Juliette's books on her website: www.julietteduncan.com/library

BLESSINGS,

Juliette

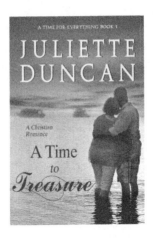

"There is a time for everything,
and a season for every activity under the heavens:
a time to be born and a time to die,
a time to plant and a time to uproot,
a time to kill and a time to heal,
a time to tear down and a time to build,
a time to weep and a time to laugh,
a time to mourn and a time to dance,
a time to scatter stones and a time to gather them,
a time to embrace and a time to refrain from embracing,
a time to search and a time to give up,
a time to keep and a time to throw away,
a time to tear and a time to mend,
a time to be silent and a time to speak,
a time to love and a time to hate,
a time for war and a time for peace."

Ecclesiastes 3:1-8

Chapter 1
Sydney, Australia
Wendy Miller rigidly held her tears in check when her

eldest daughter, Natalie, slipped on her beautiful wedding gown. The strapless A-line style suited Natalie's slim figure perfectly, but the prospect of her daughter walking down the aisle without her father brought a massive lump to Wendy's throat.

Wendy's husband, Greg, had suffered a fatal heart attack four years earlier, and although the pain she felt whenever she thought of him had lessened to a dull ache, it was moments like these that brought it rushing back.

"How does it look, Mum?" Natalie stood in front of the full-length mirror, peering over her shoulder at the back of the gown, while Roxanne, the gown's creator, made some minor adjustments.

"It's perfect, sweetheart. You're going to be a gorgeous bride."

Relief filled Natalie's face. "Thank you."

"Your father would have been so proud to walk you down the aisle in this," Wendy added in a wistful tone.

"Mum! You need to stop saying that. It's hard enough as it is."

Wendy bit her lip. Natalie was right. They were both struggling, and Natalie didn't need constant reminders that her father wouldn't be there on her special day when it no doubt was on her mind anyway. Wendy reached out and rubbed Natalie's arm. "I know, sweetheart, I'm sorry."

Natalie stood completely still while Roxanne inspected the gown, making the odd adjustment here and there. Dressed in an oversized multi-coloured loose-fitting shirt, purple tights and yellow sneakers, the young woman didn't look like one of Sydney's top fashion designers, but Roxanne Alexander was a multi-award winner eagerly sought after by the well-to-do, and they'd been fortunate to engage her services. "I won't do the final adjustments until the week before the wedding, but other than that, I think it's done," Roxanne said as she straightened.

Natalie beamed. "I love it so much. Thank you. Now all I have to do is eat salad for the next three months."

Roxanne laughed. "I wouldn't worry about that. A few extra pounds won't matter."

"Great! I wasn't looking forward to starving myself."

Wendy chuckled. Her daughter was as thin as a rake, even though she had a voracious appetite. "I don't think there's any chance of that. Come on, get dressed and I'll buy you lunch."

While Roxanne helped Natalie out of the gown, Wendy inspected the bridesmaids' dresses, which Roxanne also had designed. Paige, Wendy's youngest daughter, had been less than co-operative and showed little interest in her sister's wedding, turning up only once for a fitting. Wendy sometimes wondered if she'd even turn up for the wedding. She sighed heavily. It wasn't helpful comparing her children, but Natalie and Paige were so different. And then there was Simon...

"See you next time." Roxanne waved as Wendy and Natalie headed for the door.

"We'll look forward to it." Wendy smiled and then followed Natalie to the lift. While they waited, Wendy slipped her arm around Natalie's waist. "I'm sorry I get teary so often. It's...well, you know?"

"It's okay Mum. I understand. I wish Dad was here, too."

"I know you do, sweetheart."

The lift arrived and the doors opened. Stepping inside, they rode down the four levels, emerging into the foyer of the high-end building in downtown Sydney.

"Where would you like to go?" Wendy asked.

Natalie shrugged. "I don't mind, your choice."

"Okay. I know just the place." Wendy linked her arm through Natalie's and together they headed out into the bustling city. Taxis honked, moving like snails through the congested streets. Shoppers strolled along the footpath, chatting, pausing to look in shop windows, oblivious of the office workers weaving around them, hurrying to grab a quick mid-day meal before returning to their respective offices for the afternoon.

The aroma of freshly baked pizza wafted from an Italian restaurant, mingling with the scent of hot dogs piled high on a vendor's cart at the corner of Edward and King. "I wouldn't mind pizza," Natalie remarked, looking longingly over her shoulder while they waited for the lights to change.

"That's not really what I had in mind," Wendy said.

"What's wrong with pizza?"

Wendy laughed. "Nothing. Nothing at all. You know how much I love Italian food. I was just thinking of your waistline and your wedding dress." Wendy paused and then leaned in close to her daughter. "To be quite honest, I'm mostly worried about the mother-of-the-bride dress!"

The lights changed and Natalie giggled as they joined the crush of pedestrians crossing to the other side. They walked on in comfortable silence, Natalie seemingly content to follow Wendy, and several minutes later, they arrived at one of Wendy's favourite restaurants. One she and Greg had dined at often. Maybe it wasn't the wisest choice, but she couldn't think of a nicer place to lunch with her daughter.

When the maître d' greeted them, Wendy asked for an outdoor table.

"Of course, Mrs. Miller, follow me," the smartly dressed young woman replied.

Natalie raised a brow at her mother and walked beside her to the table on the balcony that the maître d' chose for them. After the young woman settled them in and promised to send a waiter to take their orders, Natalie leaned forward. "We didn't have to come here, Mum. It'll cost a fortune!"

"It's okay, darling. I wanted to spoil you," Wendy replied, trying hard to keep her voice steady. The restaurant had one of the best views of the harbour and the Opera House, and on this perfect spring day, the water glistening in the sunshine was just glorious. Just like the days when she and Greg came here...

"You don't need to," Natalie replied. She grew silent for a few seconds, her face paling. Grabbing Wendy's arm, she asked, "Are you okay, Mum?"

Wendy frowned. "Of course I am. What makes you think I'm not?"

"You look tired, that's all. And bringing me here..." Natalie's voice trailed away, but Wendy could see fear in her daughter's eyes.

"You wonder if I'm sick?"

"Yes."

Wendy squeezed Natalie's hand. "I'm fine. Nothing to worry about. Honestly."

"Are you sure?" Natalie asked, frowning.

"Positive!"

A male waiter approached and stopped beside the table. The two women grabbed their menus and quickly perused them.

"Are you ready to order, ladies, or shall I come back?" the well-groomed, dark-haired young man asked politely.

"Could you give us a few minutes, please?" Wendy removed her designer sunglasses and smiled at him.

"Of course." He poured two glasses of water from the jug on the table and stepped aside.

"There's no pizza on the menu," Natalie whispered loudly.

Wendy laughed. "You don't need pizza, Natalie."

"I know." Natalie chuckled. "Shall we share the paella instead?"

Wendy set her menu on the table and smiled lovingly at her daughter. "Good choice." She waved the waiter over and placed the order. After he left, she slipped her sunglasses back on, sipped her water, and studied her daughter. What would she do without Natalie? Soon, her eldest daughter would be married and have less time to spend with her mother. The thought saddened Wendy, but she knew she had to deal with it. She couldn't, but more importantly, wouldn't, impose on Natalie and Adam. The first year of marriage was such a special time. Even now, after all the years that had passed, memories of her first year with Greg filled her with such warmth. They'd had a wonderful marriage. But it was no good constantly reminiscing. Although he'd be waiting for her in the life to come, he was gone from this earth, and she had to accept that fact and try to build a new life on her own.

"Have you spoken to Simon lately?" Natalie asked.

Wendy blinked and returned her attention to Natalie. "Not for a few weeks. He's replied to a few texts, but I think he's super busy with work. Did you know he got a promotion?"

Natalie frowned again. "No. He's always busy when I call. Makes me think he doesn't want to talk to me anymore."

"You know your brother. When he doesn't want to talk, he doesn't want to talk. But when he chooses to, you can't stop him."

"Yes, but surely he can find time to talk to *you* at least once a week. You're his mother, after all."

"I've come to the conclusion that we have to give him space," Wendy replied as positively as she could, because, the truth was, she also wondered why Simon found it so hard to keep in touch, but she *was* his mother, and she wouldn't speak ill of him with his sister.

Natalie crossed her arms. "If he keeps this up much longer, I'm going to drive to his house and make him talk. I mean it!"

"Don't be like that, sweetheart. He doesn't like it when we pressure him, you know that."

"I don't understand him! You'd think with Dad gone, he'd be more attentive of you."

"I can look after myself. But I agree, it'd be lovely to see more of him."

The waiter approached and set the paella on the table between them. "Would you like me to serve?" he asked.

Wendy flashed an appreciative smile. "We'll be fine, thanks. It smells wonderful."

The waiter nodded, refilled their glasses, and wished them *bon appétit* before leaving them to their meal.

"Pass your plate, Mum," Natalie said, holding her hand out.

Wendy complied and Natalie heaped several spoons of the colourful dish onto the middle of the plate. Wendy held her hand up. "That's plenty, darling. Thank you."

"Are you sure? There's a lot here."

"Yes, that's fine."

Natalie filled her plate and then quickly scooped a huge spoonful into her mouth, releasing a pleasurable sigh. Wendy was glad the conversation about Simon had been dropped. His lack of communication did worry her, and she often wondered if something was wrong, but didn't want Natalie concerned about him with her wedding fast approaching. Wendy decided to call him again when she got home.

After making quick work of the paella, Natalie leaned back in her chair and placed her hands across her stomach. "So, what have you decided about the trip?"

Wendy sipped her iced tea and released a long sigh. Greg's grandmother, who lived just south of London, was turning ninety, and Wendy had booked a trip to the U.K. to attend the celebration. She'd also invited her friend, Robyn, to accompany her, but now Robyn couldn't go because her mother had taken ill, and Wendy was considering cancelling. She set her glass on the table and toyed with her fork. "I don't think I'll go."

"Oh Mum, I think you should. Since Dad's death, you've hardly taken a holiday—I think it'll do you good."

"But on my own?"

Natalie chuckled. "You never know, you might meet a handsome gentleman who'll sweep you off your feet!"

"Natalie!"

"Sorry..." A playful grin had spread across Natalie's face. She leaned forward, crossing her arms on the table. "Seriously, I think you should go. You've travelled a lot, you'll be fine. You need to go, Mum."

Wendy sighed heavily. "I'll give it some more thought. If I stay home, I can help more with the wedding preparations."

"You've already done more than enough. It's all in hand," Natalie replied with just a hint of exasperation in her voice.

"I know. But it seems strange to think of travelling to the other side of the world without your dad. It won't be the same."

Natalie squeezed her mother's hand. "I know. But go. Do it for Dad."

Wendy grimaced and swallowed the lump in her throat. "I'll think about it, but right now, I think I'd like coffee. Would you like one?"

"That would be lovely. Thank you."

Wendy beckoned the waiter over and ordered two cups.

"And can I tempt you with the dessert menu?" He quirked a brow as he held out two.

Wendy smiled politely. "Thank you, but no. Coffee will be fine."

Natalie leaned forward again after the waiter left, her face filled with disappointment. "I was going to order something," she said in a sulky tone.

Wendy chuckled, shaking her head. "You do take after your father with your sweet tooth."

"I can't help it," Natalie replied defensively, but then she laughed.

"I guess not. But even though Roxanne said it didn't matter, you should still watch what you're eating." Wendy quickly bit her lip. She shouldn't have said that. Natalie was a grown woman and could make her own decisions about what to eat and what to avoid. Thank goodness Natalie had an understanding nature. Paige would never have let her get away with saying anything like that. "I'm sorry darling. Have whatever you want." Wendy smiled and beckoned the waiter again.

———

CEDAR SPRINGS RANCH, TEXAS

Bruce McCarthy swung his legs off the bed and glanced at his watch. *Three p.m.* Releasing a slow breath, he ran his hand over his still thick, but graying hair. He really had to stop falling asleep in the afternoons—it was such a waste of time. However, now his eldest son, Nate, was running the ranch and insisted he take it easy, Bruce often found his eyes drooping in the early afternoon following their substantial mid-day meal, and he usually succumbed to a nap. However, he wasn't tired—he was just bored.

At sixty-three years of age, Bruce wasn't old, but his brush with bowel cancer a year earlier had shaken his sons, especially Nate. Although he'd beaten the disease, Nate had placed him on light duties, but Bruce was bored to tears. Retirement didn't suit him. He'd much rather be out tending cattle instead of looking after the books, which had never been one of his strong points.

A tentative knock sounded on the door. "Dad..." It was Nate, whispering in a low voice.

"Come in, son." Bruce pushed to his feet and crossed the room, grabbing a bottle of water from a small refrigerator tucked in a corner.

The door opened and Nate poked his rugged, good-looking cowboy head inside. "I'm heading to the bank in a few minutes. Need anything?"

Bruce shook his head. "I'm fine, thanks. I'm going to town soon, anyway."

Nate's forehead creased. "Sure you're up to it?"

Bruce did his best to hide his annoyance at his son's remark. He didn't need molly-coddling—the doctor had given him a clean bill of health. If only Nate wouldn't worry so much. And it was only a meeting at church to discuss fund-raising for the upgrade of the children's ministry hall. He wasn't about to do the actual renovations. "Of course I'm up to it," he replied with a reassuring smile before taking a slug of water. He didn't mention to Nate the other thing he was doing in town. He'd save that for later, when it was all sorted and too late to do anything about.

After Nate closed the door, Bruce sat at his desk and opened the drawer, taking out the itinerary the young woman at the travel agency had drawn up for him a few days earlier. He'd sworn her to secrecy. If Nate knew he was planning a trip to Ireland and England on his own, Bruce knew it was unlikely he'd even reach the airport lounge, let alone board the plane. But could he do it? He'd always thought that when he retired, he and his wife, Faith, would travel the world together, but Faith had passed on ten years earlier. Now, the choice was to go on his own or not at all.

Bruce re-read the itinerary. First stop, Ireland, the land of his forebears. His grandfather, Edward Bruce McCarthy, emigrated from Ireland in his early twenties, bought Cedar Springs Ranch and never returned. However, he never forgot his homeland and told endless tales and stories about the beautiful green isle. Ireland, Edward had told his young grandson, was a land filled with poets and fables, dreamers and agitators. Edward had sown a seed in the young Bruce's mind, and he wanted to see it for himself. He'd recently decided that now was the perfect time to visit the land he'd heard so much about, and maybe try to find some family members at the same time.

To Bruce it made perfect sense to go. He wasn't needed on the ranch, and after his health scare, every day was a blessing, and he wanted to make the most of the precious gift of life. Yes, he'd do it. He'd make the booking, pay for it, and then tell the family.

––––––––

AFTER DROPPING Natalie outside her apartment block, Wendy continued on to her home at Cremorne, a suburb on the northern side of Sydney Harbour. It still was, and always had been, a lovely family home. She and Greg bought it soon after they married and had raised their children there. However, the memories could sometimes be overwhelming and the sprawling three-level home with views over the glistening harbour seemed so big and quiet now that only she and Paige lived there. But since Paige was rarely at home, it was almost as if Wendy lived alone, and that made the house seem even larger and emptier.

She turned her car into the driveway, waved to Rose, her elderly neighbour who looked up from her gardening and smiled, and then drove into the double garage. Stepping out of the car, the boxes stacked against one side of the garage wall caught Wendy's attention. Simon's... She let out a sigh. Would he ever collect them? She'd given him several ultimatums but hadn't the heart to follow through with tossing his things out when he hadn't come for them by the appointed date. She sighed again and unlocked the internal door leading to the house. It didn't matter. It wasn't as if the space was being used for anything else. Paige didn't have a car, and Wendy had finally sold Greg's large SUV just last year, so there really was no need to hassle Simon.

Pushing the door open, Wendy stepped into the house, set her bag on the kitchen counter, and filled the kettle. A faint meow sounded from the sunroom, and moments later, Muffin, Wendy's large, fluffy Persian, rubbed against her legs. Wendy bent down and picked him up, gave him a cuddle, and then set him back on the floor while she made a cup of tea.

After turning on some background music to cover the silence that always filled the rambling house these days, she carried her tea to the sunroom and sat in her favourite chair. Muffin immediately joined her and settled on her lap.

Opening the book she'd begun the night before, Wendy began reading while sipping her tea. She soon closed it when she found herself re-reading the same paragraph several times. Her focus was elsewhere. Having all but decided to cancel the trip to

London, the conversation with Natalie now had her mind awhirl. Maybe she should go. Could Natalie be right, that it might do her good? Her gaze travelled to the large family photo on the far wall, taken not long before Greg passed away unexpectedly. They all looked so happy, and they *had* been. Such a different story now. Paige hadn't coped well with her father's sudden death and blamed God for letting him die before his time. Simon had withdrawn further. Natalie did what she always did and soldiered on. They all had their own ways of coping. Wendy drew comfort and strength from quiet times spent in the Word, her family, her church, and her work as a part-time University Lecturer. But she still missed Greg terribly. She guessed she always would.

She reached for the travel pack the agent had given her and flicked through the itinerary. She and Robyn had planned to visit Ireland before flying to England. Greg had always wanted to visit the emerald isle. Wendy wasn't sure what had sparked his interest, but he'd always promised they'd go, and she'd been looking forward to seeing it. But could she do it on her own? Would it make her miss him more, or would it help her let go and move on? She drew a deep breath and closed her eyes, fingering the cross around her neck. *Lord, I'm really struggling with this—please show me what to do. You know how much I miss Greg, and how heavy my heart is when I think about travelling to the other side of the world without him, but maybe I should go. Please help me draw strength from You, and please guide and direct me. In Jesus' precious name. Amen.*

Half an hour later, after finishing her tea and finally finishing a chapter of her book, inexplicable peace flooded Wendy's heart. She made up her mind. She'd go to the birthday party in London, and to Ireland. She'd do it for Greg, but also for herself. She needed to start making a life for herself without him, because deep down, she knew that the loneliness that was her constant companion wouldn't leave until she did. Clinging to memories, as wonderful as they were, wouldn't help her move forward. Taking this trip, no matter how challenging it might be, would be a start to building a new life. Drawing a resolved breath, she picked up the phone and called the travel agent.

Continue to read "A Time to Treasure" by grabbing your copy http://www.julietteduncan.com/linkspage/389303.

OTHER POTTER'S HOUSE BOOKS

Find all of the Potter's House Books at:

http://pottershousebooks.com/our-books/

OTHER BOOKS BY JULIETTE DUNCAN

Find all of Juliette Duncan's books on her website:
www.julietteduncan.com/library

THE TRUE LOVE SERIES

Immerse yourself into the lives of Ben, Tessa and Jayden...

After her long-term relationship falls apart, Tessa Scott is left questioning God's plan for her life, and is feeling vulnerable and unsure of how to move forward. Ben Williams is struggling to keep the pieces of his life together after his wife of fourteen years walks out on him and their teenage son.

Stephanie, Tessa's housemate, knows the pain both Tessa and Ben have suffered. When she inadvertently sets up a meeting between them, there's no denying that they are drawn to each other, but will that mutual attraction do more harm than good?

Can Tessa and Ben let go of their leftover baggage and examine their feelings in order to follow a new path? Are they prepared for the road ahead, regardless of the challenges? Will they trust God to equip them with all they need for the journey ahead?

"Since reading the Shadows Series, I've been hooked on Juliette Duncan's writing. Tender Love is another example of her talent for bringing characters to life and weaving a story with all the elements of superior storytelling.

Totally clean, yet written with adult situations; the pain of breakups, broken marriages, rearing teenagers, job challenges, maintaining relationships with parents and friends. And in the center of the story, we find two people who, while recuperating from painful situations in their personal lives, find hope and love, looking forward into their future together. The scriptures and Biblical principles are so masterfully worked into the book, they complement the story, rather than pull us away, as some, less talented writers sometimes do. This is not a long read, but one which will satisfy." Amazon Customer

The Precious Love Series

Best read after "The True Love Series" but can be read separately

Book 1 - Forever Cherished

Now Tessa's dream of living in the country has been realized, she wants to share her and Ben's blessings with others, but when a sad, lonely woman comes to stay, Tessa starts to think she's bitten off more than she can chew, and has to rely on her faith at every turn.

Leah Maloney is carrying a truck-load of disappointments from the past and has almost given up on life. Her older sister arranges for her to spend time at 'Misty Morn', but Leah is suspicious of her sister's motives.

"Forever Cherished" is a stand-alone novel, but is better read as a follow-on from "The True Love Series" books.

Book 2 - Forever Faithful

Although half a world separates them, Jayden Williams has never stopped loving Angela Morgan, the green-eyed, red haired girl who captured his heart and led him to the Lord in the hills of Montana several years earlier.

When he becomes the victim of a one-punch attack and is lying unconscious in a hospital bed half-way around the world, Angela knows she has no choice but to go to him. What if he died and she wasn't there for him? She'd never forgive herself.

But Angela has a boyfriend who isn't happy about her friendship with Jayden. When her boyfriend arrives on Jayden's grandparents' doorstep unannounced, Angela has to decide if her friendship with Jayden is stronger than her love for Cole. Can she leave Jayden like Cole wants her to and risk losing his love?

Will God answer her prayers and restore Jayden to health, or will she need to accept the outcome as God's will, whether he lives or dies?

Book 3 - Forever His

A honeymoon made in heaven, a family fractured by fraud...

Following their romantic beach wedding in Hawaii, Jayden and Angie embark on the honeymoon of a lifetime - the Himalayas, the Taj Mahal, the Great Wall, Angkor Wat, the Greek islands...the list goes on.

Fun and challenge await the young couple at every turn, but Angie soon discovers that Jayden is a risk taker, and she has no choice but to go along with him.

But does she embrace the challenge or put her foot down?

And what happens after their honeymoon comes to an end? Angie wants to settle in Hunter's Hollow, Montana. Jayden wants to settle in Maryvale, Queensland. It's an impossible situation. Will God show them where He wants them to live, and if He does, will they listen?

Meanwhile, trouble is brewing back home. Jayden's father, Ben, is in trouble. His boss has been accused of fraud, and although upright, conservative and God fearing, Ben is entangled...

Tessa, his wife, is worried he might slip back into the depression that's haunted him for most of his life.

They've been through so much, and God has been with them through it all, but can they trust Him now when so much is at stake? When it's possible they could lose their beloved property, 'Misty Morn', *but worse still, Ben could go to jail?*

A heartwarming and uplifting continuation to the "Precious Love Series", this contemporary Christian romance can be read as a stand-alone novel, but is better read as part of the series.

The Shadows Series

An inspirational romance, a story of passion and love, and of God's inexplicable desire to free people from pasts that haunt them so they can live a life full of His peace, love and forgiveness, regardless of the circumstances. *"Lingering Shadows"* is set in England, and follows the story of Lizzy, a headstrong, impulsive young lady from a privileged background, and Daniel, a roguish Irishman who sweeps her off her feet. But can Lizzy leave the shadows of her past behind and give Daniel the love he deserves, and will Daniel find freedom and release in God?

Praise for "The Shadows Series"

"I absolutely LOVE this series. I grew to connect with each of the characters with each passing page. If you are looking for a story with real-life situations & great character development, with the love of God interwoven throughout the pages, I HIGHLY recommend The Shadows Series Box Set by Juliette Duncan!" JLB

"Amazing story, one of the best I have ever read. Gives us so much information regarding alcoholism and abusive behavior. It also gives us understanding on

how to respond. The Bible was well presented to assist with understanding how to accomplish the behaviors necessary to deal with the situations." *Jeane M*

"This boxed set deeply stirred my soul and thrilled my spirit as God spoke and moved over the despair of alcoholism, Irish tempers, and loss of loved ones." *Sharon*

The Madeleine Richards Series

Although the 3 book series is intended mainly for pre-teen/Middle Grade girls, it's been read and enjoyed by people of all ages. Here's what one reader had to say about it: "*Juliette has a fabulous way of bringing her characters to life. Maddy is at typical teenager with authentic views and actions that truly make it feel like you are feeling her pain and angst. You want to enter into her situation and make everything better. Mom and soon to be dad respond to her with love and gentle persuasion while maintaining their faith and trust in Jesus, whom they know, will give them wisdom as they continue on their lives journey. Appropriate for teenage readers but any age can enjoy." Amazon Reader*

Hank and Sarah - A Love Story

The Prequel to "The Madeleine Richards Series" is a FREE thank you gift for joining my mailing list. www.julietteduncan.com/subscribe

The Potter's House Books...stories of hope, redemption, and second chances. Find out more here:

http://pottershousebooks.com/our-books/

The Homecoming

Kayla McCormack is a famous pop-star, but her life is a mess. Dane Carmichael has a disability, but he has a heart for God. He had a crush on her at school, but she doesn't remember him. His simple faith and life fascinate her, But can she surrender her life of fame and fortune to find true love?

Unchained

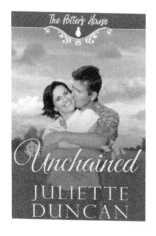

Imprisoned by greed – redeemed by love

Sally Richardson has it all. A devout, hard-working, well-respected husband, two great kids, a beautiful home, wonderful friends. Her life is perfect. Until it isn't.

When Brad Richardson, accountant, business owner, and respected church member, is sentenced to five years in jail, Sally is shell-shocked. How had she not known about her husband's fraudulent activity? And how, as an upstanding member of their tight-knit community, did he ever think he'd get away with it? He's defrauded clients, friends, and fellow church members. She doubts she can ever trust him again.

Locked up with murderers and armed robbers, Brad knows that the only way to survive his incarceration is to seek God with all his heart - something he should have done years ago. But how does he convince his family that his remorse is genuine? Will they ever forgive him?

He's failed them. But most of all, he's failed God. His poor decisions have ruined this once perfect family.

They've lost everything they once held dear. Will they lose each other as well?

Stand Alone Christian Romantic Suspense

Leave Before He Kills You

When his face grew angry, I knew he could murder...

That face drove me and my three young daughters to flee across Australia.

I doubted he'd ever touch the girls, but if I wanted to live and see them grow, I had to do something.

The plan my friend had proposed was daring and bold, but it also gave me hope.

My heart thumped. What if he followed?

Radical, honest and real, this Christian romantic suspense is one woman's journey to freedom you won't put down...get your copy and read it now.

A Time for Everything Series

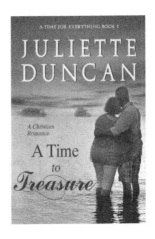

A Time to Treasure

She lost her husband and misses him dearly. He lost his wife but is ready to move on. Will a chance meeting in a foreign city change their lives forever?

Following her husband's untimely death, Wendy Miller's life revolves around her adult children, but when she accepts an invitation to her late husband's grandmother's 90th birthday party in London, she meets a dashing, silver-haired Texan cowboy in Dublin. Bruce captures her heart, but can she move past the memories of her late husband and truly open her heart all over again?

Bruce McCarthy did his best to hold his family and ranch together after his wife died in a car accident ten years before, but following a recent health scare, he decides to live every day as if it were his last and books a flight to Ireland to find his Irish family.

The captivating woman he accidentally spills coffee on one morning stirs something inside him, and Bruce wonders if God might be giving him a second chance at love...

As they meet again in London, Paris and Venice, their friendship grows deeper, but while Bruce is eager to take their friendship further, Wendy is unsure if her adult children will accept a new man in her life, especially when one of them still blames God for allowing her father to die prematurely.

If Wendy can trust God to take care of the details, and Bruce can overcome his fears of his cancer returning, then they may just find true love again after all...

A Time to Treasure is the first book in The Time For Everything Series, a set of contemporary Christian romance novels set in Sydney, Australia, and Texas, USA. If you like real-life characters, faith-filled families, and friendships that become something more, then you'll love Juliette Duncan's inspirational second-chance romance.

ABOUT THE AUTHOR

Juliette Duncan is passionate about writing true to life Christian romances that will touch her readers' hearts and make a difference in their lives. Drawing on her own often challenging real-life experiences, Juliette writes deeply emotional stories that highlight God's amazing love and faithfulness, for which she's eternally grateful. Juliette lives in Brisbane, Australia. She and her husband have five adult children and seven grandchildren whom they love dearly, as well as an elderly long-haired dachshund and a little black cat. When not writing, Juliette and her husband love exploring the great outdoors.

Connect with Juliette:
Email: author@julietteduncan.com
Website: www.julietteduncan.com
Facebook: www.facebook.com/JulietteDuncanAuthor
BookBub: www.bookbub.com/authors/juliette-duncan